J.L. POWERS

THIS THING CALLED
THE FUTURE

J.L. POWERS

THIS THING CALLED
THE FUTURE

Cinco Puntos Press

WWW.CINCOPUNTOS.COM

This Thing Called the Future
Copyright © 2011 by J.L. Powers

Cover photo by Izak de Vries.

Printed in the U.S.

First Edition
10 9 8 7 6 5 4 3 2 1

LIBRARY OF CONGRESS CATALOGING-IN-PUBLICATION DATA

Powers, J. L. (Jessica Lynn), 1974-
  This thing called the future / by J.L. Powers—1st ed.
     p. cm.
Summary: Fourteen-year-old Khosi's mother wants her to get an education to break
out of their South African shantytown, although she herself is wasting away from an
untreated illness, while Khosi's grandmother, Gogo, seeks help from a traditional
Zulu healer.
ISBN 978-1-933693-95-8 (cloth) / ISBN 978-1-947627-10-9 (paper)
ISBN 978-1-935955-10-8 (e-book)
 [1. Sick—Fiction. 2. Healers—Fiction. 3. Medical care—Fiction. 4. Mothers and
daughters—Fiction. 5. Zulu (African people)—Fiction. 6. Blacks—South Africa—Fiction. 7. South Africa—Fiction.] I. Title.
 PZ7.P883443Thi 2011
 [Fic]—dc22

2010037399

Cover and book design by Antonio Castro H.
Compositing by Elena Marinaccio & Lee Byrd

Elena is long gone to the big city, had two girls, now half grown,
and I'm surrounded by grands.
Where has the time gone?

PART ONE

THE WITCH

CHAPTER ONE

Nightmare

A drumbeat wakes me. *Ba-Boom. Ba-Boom.* It is beating a funeral dirge.

When I was my little sister Zi's age, we rarely heard those drums. Now they wake me so many Saturdays. It seems somebody is dying all the time. These drums are calling our next-door neighbor, Baba Dudu, to leave this place and join the ancestors where they live, in the earth, the land of the shadows.

I get up and walk to the window, peeking through the curtain at the Dudus' house in the faint pink light of dawn. Their house is small like ours, government built—a matchbox house made of crumbling cement and peeling peach-colored paint. It is partially obscured by the huge billboard the government put up some few weeks ago between our houses. This is what it announces in bold white lettering against a black background:

THIS YEAR, **100,000** CHILDREN
WILL BE BORN WITH HIV!

Gogo, my grandmother, fretted like mad when that billboard went up. "People who can't read, they will just see that symbol for AIDS right over our house, and they will say, 'Those people, they are the ones spreading it.'"

I tried to soothe her. "People know better than that. Those billboards are everywhere." It's true, the government wants everyone to know about the disease of these days before we all die from it.

But Gogo shook her head. "You watch, we will have bad luck from this thing," she predicted.

Ba-Boom. Ba-Boom. The drums next door continue and a dog across the street howls in response.

I look for movement in the Dudus' yard but see nothing.

Like us, they have wrapped thick barbed wire around the top of their fence in order to keep *tsotsis* away. Only some few of us have anything that *tsotsis* would steal. But these days, things are so hard those gangsters will hold a gun to your head and steal crumbs of *phuthu* right out of your mouth even as you are chewing and swallowing.

Ba-Boom. Ba-Boom. Two women, walking down the dirt road that runs in front of our house and balancing heavy bags of mealie-meal on their heads, pause to stare at the Dudus' house.

I look back at my sleeping family. Zi and Gogo share one bed, low snores erupting from Gogo's open mouth, revealing reddened gums where her teeth have rotted and fallen out over the years. Mama looks peaceful in the bed that she and I share when she comes home.

During the week, Mama lives in Greytown, where she works as a schoolteacher. She doesn't make enough money for us to live with her, so she rents a very tiny room there and sends the rest of the money home, which supplements Gogo's government pension. My *baba* lives with his mother in Durban, another city an hour away. Unlike Mama, he doesn't have a good job; there is hardly ever enough money to go see him.

All over South Africa, people struggle. *Nobody* has enough money. Anyway, we *blacks* don't have money. Whitesssmaybe they are rich, but the rest of us suffer. There are poor whites, it's true, but not so many as poor blacks.

Even the next door neighbor, MaDudu, she will suffer now that her husband has died. This week, Mama came home from her job some few days early to help with her husband's insurance settlement. "Yo! It is sad, he left her very little money," Mama said.

"What is she going to do?" I asked. "How is she going to live?"

"She has six grown children," Mama said. "They will help her."

"How?" Gogo asked. "They don't have any education so they don't even have good jobs."

"She is old. She has a government pension," Mama said.

Gogo clucked her tongue. "It is not enough. I don't know how we would manage if you did not work. We will have to be very good to her and help her if she needs it."

Gogo is always generous with what little we have. "If we don't help others, what will happen to us when we are the ones needing help?" she asks.

Ba-boom. Ba-boom. I can't believe my family is sleeping through the racket.

To me, the drumbeat is foreboding. After my uncle Jabulani died, my *baba's* family was almost torn apart by the accusations until they called a *sangoma* in. She consulted the ancestors and told them that in this case, there had been no witchcraft, only the disease of these days. "It is just the sadness of today," she said, "that the young people are dying and leaving their children without parents."

"Leave the curtain and come back to bed, Khosi," Mama murmurs. She pulls back the covers and pats the space beside her.

"The beating of the drums woke me," I say. "Can't you hear it?"

"It's too much early," Mama replies, yawning loud.

"It's a funeral and you know what that means," I say. "Trouble."

"He was an old man and ready to die, Khosi," she says. "Nobody is going to say his death was this thing of witchcraft. It isn't like all these young people dying before it is their time. *That* is what worries everybody."

It's true, what she says. When a young person dies, it is because their spirit was taken from them. But an old man's death is natural and nothing to fear. He has lived his life and it is time for him to become an ancestor, to help his descendants through life.

"*Woza*, Khosi," Mama says again.

So I let the curtain fall and crawl back into bed. Mama puts her arm around me and I cuddle up into her fat cocoa-brown warmth.

Her orange headscarf tickles my forehead as I drift back into the world of dreams, the drumbeat troubling me even in sleep. This one is a white dream, the color of the moon in the afternoon sky, so I know the ancestors sent it to me.

I'm sitting in hospital with Mama. Her skin is weeping underneath a white bandage. "They're going to remove the burnt skin," she explains when I wonder why we're here, especially when I see all the bodies of dead people piled up in the corner.

We wait for a long time and finally they call her into a small room. The nurse comes to remove Mama's bandages, her gloves bloody from the last patient.

Mama jerks her arm away. "No, Sisi, I do not want you to do this until you change your gloves."

The nurse crosses her arms. "Listen here, I have been working at this hospital for fifteen years. Are you going to tell me how to do my job?"

"That last man you treated could have AIDS," Mama says.

The nurse storms out of the room. Mama takes the nurse's instruments and begins to scrape the dead skin off. "You see, this is why we need good nurses in South Africa," she tells me. "Otherwise, they just do this thing of spreading HIV."

The dream changes and now we're sitting in church as the collection plate is being passed around. When it reaches us, Zi carefully places the five *rands* that Gogo gave her in the plate, looking proud and happy that she's giving to the church.

I pass the collection plate to Mama and watch as she starts to put a twenty *rand* note inside, then stops, clutching the money before passing the plate on by.

"Mama?" I whisper, surprised. Mama always gives to the church. *It is our duty and obligation as Christians*, she has always said. *If we fail to give to the church, which feeds our souls, it is stealing from God.*

"Hush, Khosi, we need it to pay the medical bills," Mama says, and I notice that her bandage is bloody and weeping a thick yellow substance. She sees the look on my face. "It is just a little thing, Khosi," she says. "God understands we need the money."

I wake, a taste in my mouth that comes only after dreaming. And my shoulders ache, like I have been lifting heavy bags all night long.

I know that dreams are not exactly what they seem. But I also know that to dream is to see the truth at night. You may think one thing during the day, but find out it's a lie when you dream. *Sangomas* hear the voices of the ancestors all the time, but night is when their spirits speak to all of us, even we regular folks.

What are the ancestors trying to tell me?

CHAPTER TWO

ENCOUNTER

Gogo leaves the house for two things only: church and funerals. Today it's our neighbor's funeral. While I cook *phuthu* for breakfast, she clucks around the house, grumbling. "Every Saturday, another funeral," she says. "It is too much sadness."

"Yes, another funeral and another day of listening to lies," Mama says, as if she is agreeing with Gogo.

"What do you mean, Mama?" I am busy wiping the counter, even the parts where chunks are missing. When I'm done, I start to sweep the floor. It's a difficult job. The floor is uneven, with ridges that make it hard to sweep dirt away.

"You watch, at the funeral, they will make Umnumzana Dudu out to be such a kind man," Mama says. "But he'd get his paycheck, go to the *shebeen*, and come home drunk. Then he would beat his children and wife. We could hear the cries, every month. You remember? It is always that way at funerals, we say what we wish had been, not what really was. At *my* funeral!"

"Elizabeth!" Gogo hushes her, quick quick. "You are just talk talk talk. Don't speak of your death; it's bad luck."

Mama laughs. "God already knows the day and hour of my death, Mama," she says. "There is nothing *anyone* can do about it."

Gogo shakes her head at Mama's foolishness. "Witches might hear you," she says. "They have the power to steal life before it is your time."

"But that doesn't bother me, hey," Mama says. "I'm a Christian." She sounds almost smug when she says this.

Mama and Gogo argue about this all the time. Mama believes in the things of white men, science and God only. She says the only power witches have over us is our fear. But Gogo says there is *African* science too, and the white man's science knows nothing about these things.

Na mina? I agree with Gogo. All my life, I have seen and heard things I can't explain. Like the dream the ancestors sent me last night.

"I'm a Christian too," Gogo mumbles as Mama disappears into the bathroom to get ready for the funeral. "There are witches in the Bible," she reminds me. "It is not only because I'm an old woman and foolish that I believe these things."

"I know, Gogo," I say, soothing her as I button her black funeral dress. She doesn't like being helpless, as though she is just Zi's age. She tries to help, fumbling with each button until I reach it. But her fingers are too gnarled and weak from arthritis.

When Mama and Gogo are dressed in their funeral finery, we set out to walk up the hill to the Zionist church where the Dudus worship. Mama looks so amazing in a lacy black dress and a black hat with roses attached, her bosom spilling out of her dress. I hope I am as beautiful as Mama when I dress up!

We walk up the dirt road, dodging chickens and taxis that roar past, trickling loud *kwaito* music, the side door open and the fare collector looking at us with a question in his eyes. *Do you need a ride?* We shake our heads and each taxi zooms by, seeking other customers, beats blaring— *doof doof doof!* through the township.

Ahead of us, Zi clings to Mama's hand and looks up at her as she chatters away, wanting her attention one hundred percent.

I walk beside Gogo, towering over her. I'm not a tall girl but Gogo's so short and bent over, the top of her head only reaches my chest. I put my arm around her as we walk, to help her up the hill.

"It is too much hard, this hill," she puffs.

"Why don't you rest just now?" I say. "There is no hurry."

Gogo smiles, revealing her missing front teeth. She leans against a tree stump, catching her breath.

Halfway up the hill, we can look out over the dirt roads running up and down through Imbali's hills. Smoke rises from thousands of small houses and shacks crowded together, as far as the eye can see. Just beyond is the city of Pietermaritzburg, shrouded in early morning smog. Imbali was created for we blacks by the government, during the time of apartheid. Only whites could live in the city during those days, so we lived in these sprawling townships hidden off the main roads and just outside the city limits. Now, of course, we can live wherever we want—but most of us can't afford to live anywhere else.

When Gogo has stopped breathing so hard we start walking again. I try to talk so that Gogo doesn't feel like she has to. I just let words fall out of my mouth while Gogo struggles the rest of the way up the hill.

But I fall silent as soon as we reach the witch's house, a big house at the top of the hill. Gogo leans heavily on my arm. We both look at the dirt, hoping we won't accidentally make eye contact with the old woman who lives there.

Ever since I was a child, Gogo has warned me about her. "Khosi, there are women in this world who want to hurt you," she would say. And the woman who lived in this house was one of those women. "She is *too* much powerful. You must watch out, hey!"

Gogo always spoke in hushed tones when she talked about her. The dog lying in the sun, the chicken pecking in the dirt, the fly buzzing around your head—*they could be her spies.* And who knew what she would do if she heard you talking about her?

"She has a maze of tunnels underneath her house," Gogo would whisper. "They lead to gigantic gold mines. She kidnaps people on the streetímen, women, even children. She turns those people into zombies. At night, she makes her zombies go deep into those tunnels to look for gold. *That* is how she makes all her money."

Gogo had always warned me that you couldn't recognize a witch by the way she dressed or even the way she behaved. *Anybody* can be a witch. Your own mother can be a witch and you won't even know it!

Now that I am fourteen, I sometimes wonder if Gogo is right about everything she says. But I do know she's right about this old woman. Whenever I've passed her on the streets, she cackles like she knows all my secrets. I don't dare look at her, afraid if I do, I'll be sucked in by her power and become one of her zombies.

Today as we hurry by, we're both startled by a sudden rattling sound. Looking up, I see that old woman grabbing hold of her fence and shaking it to get our attention.

"Nomkhosi Zulu," she calls.

How does she know my name? We look at each other. Her eyes grip and hold me firm, the way her fingers clutch the metal fence. There are gold flecks deep in her eyes, and a large gold tooth glints as she spreads her lips into a thin grin.

"I've been watching you, Nomkhosi Zulu." Her voice is honey sweet. "Ever since you were a little girl."

There's a strange rhythm to her words. They echo in my mind, a song playing over and over—and oh, how I *want* to dance.

"Hey, *wena Ntombi!* Come here, sweet thing." There's something about her voice...Why, she sounds like she has stolen Gogo's voice.

Gogo sucks in her breath and grabs my elbow, her wordless plea, *Masihambe, Khosi. We must run.*

But I'm drawn to the fence, an ant marching to sugar. The old woman reaches through the wire, seizing my arm in her wrinkled fingers, her grasp rough, her fingernails digging in until I gasp.

"This one's spirit is strong," she says.

"Khosi." Gogo's voice is low but strong. "We must go now."

But I'm like a doll in this old woman's hands.

"Khosi," Gogo says, now more urgent.

The old woman lets go suddenly, almost shoving me backwards. "*Yebo, hamba.*" Her mouth breaks open into a wide grin. "Yes, go now with your weak old *gogo*. But I will come for you just now, Nomkhosi Zulu. Soon, I will come for you." Her laughter twists and coils, snake-like and cold. "And nothing on *this* earth can stop me."

I stumble against Gogo, who puts her arm around me. She is shaking, even more badly than I am. We hurry away, not daring to look back.

It isn't until we're around the curve and out of the old woman's sight that we stop to look at my arm, bleeding from where her fingernails dug in.

"Oh, no," I moan. If a witch is able to get some of your body dirt from your clothing or your skin, she has the power to harm you.

I breathe deep before asking the burning question. "Do you think that old woman will really come for me? Is she really a witch, like you say, Gogo?"

"*Angaz'*, Khosi," Gogo says. She looks as worried as I feel. "We will ask the *sangoma* to make some *muthi* to protect you."

The right *muthi* can protect you from all sorts of evil. But in the wrong hands, that same *muthi* can be used against you. You have to be vigilant-and hope and pray that both God and the spirits of your ancestors are strong with you.

"What will Mama say?"

"Eh-he, I don't know." Gogo's hands still tremble as she holds onto me, her energy dwindling as if the old woman has already consumed her strength. That's what witches do, after all. They suck the life out of people, to make themselves rich or to make themselves live longer. "She is not believing in the old ways. It will be difficult even now to convince her that we must go to the *sangoma* about this problem."

"Mama is never here," I point out.

Gogo nods and we silently agree to keep Mama in the dark about this. We walk, quiet and tired. The whole world looks washed out, like a grainy black and white photo—the kind of photo published in history textbooks that shows early missionaries to Natal, as this part of South Africa was known then, with the first Zulu converts, formal and stiff in their European clothes.

I sneak a sideways glance at Gogo. "I wish that woman didn't know my name."

"*Yebo, impela*," Gogo agrees.

Your name is all a witch needs to have power over you.

"Gogo, how can that woman have so much power when she is so evil?"

Gogo's eyes grow dark, and I can see within them the memory of growing up in the shadow of the white man, when their power over Africans was absolute. "At the end of time, God will defeat all evil," she says. "But in the meantime, we must suffer. Perhaps this suffering is cleansing us from our sins."

"What did she mean when she said, 'This one's spirit is strong'?"

"Yo, Khosi! I have always known that," Gogo says. "You were born the same day your grandfather Babamkhulu died. I believe he gave you part of his spirit as he departed. Even then, I told your mother, '*Isithunzi sake* is strong, you watch. Khosi won't be like us. Her spirit won't stay the same all her life—it'll grow with time.' And up to this day, you look just like Babamkhulu. This to me says I am not wrong."

In the picture we have above the mantelpiece, Babamkhulu looks like an old black bird, shrewd with very dark skin, small eyes, and a beaky nose. Do I really look like him? I've always wanted to look like Mama, beautiful with smooth brown skin and wide, full lips, a big bosom and hips that sway like a tree when she dances.

"Maybe Babamkhulu's spirit will keep you safe now," Gogo says. She clasps my arm and rubs the spot where the witch dug in with her claws.

"Maybe," I say. I don't feel like my *isithunzi* is strong. I don't feel like there is anything of Babamkhulu about me. I'm just a teenage girl, vulnerable like anybody to the evil spirits that are invisible but hovering in the air all around us.

CHAPTER THREE

MAD CRUSH

After Gogo and Mama disappear into the Zionist church, I almost turn around and run home. But I could never outrun a witch. All she needs to do is hop on her baboon and come racing after me. So I keep my pace slow and deliberate, like I'm not afraid of anything.

Zi is like a tiny bolt of lightning, bristling energy as she skips ahead of me down the dirt road, whirling back and forth from house to house, going right up to each fence. Dogs bound out, hurtling toward her, barking furiously.

"Khosi! Khosi! They're coming to get me!" she screeches as they slam against the fence, the thin wire trembling under their weight. Zi throws her arms around me, thrilled with terror, her black eyes happy-scared as she looks up at me.

The people smile indulgently at us as we pass.

"What will you do if one of these dogs escapes?" I ask, scolding her a little. Because Mama is gone throughout the week, and because Gogo is so old, I can't help but be Zi's second mother. Besides, it takes my mind off everything else. "What if it comes running out and tries to bite you?"

"Then I'll make friends with it," she says.

I laugh. That is exactly what Zi would do too. She makes friends with everybody and everything. When Zi settles down and stays beside me, clinging to my hand, I ask her something that's bothering me. "Zi, do you think I look like Babamkhulu?"

"How do I know? I've never met Babamkhulu," she says.

"You've seen his picture on the mantel."

She screws up her little face as if she's trying to remember. "*You* look like Khosi," she decides. "*Babamkhulu* looks like *you*!"

Maybe I should have known better than to ask a little girl to reassure me that I'm beautiful.

We reach the tuck shop, a small shack built in front of the owner's house and stocked with small items—biscuits, bread, milk, oranges, cool drinks. When I see the man sitting on a red bucket in front of the shop, tipped back and leaning against its tin wall, looking as though he's been enjoying too much beer at Mama Thambo's *shebeen*, I look around to see if other people are nearby. But the street is empty.

It's true, drunk men are everywhere in Imbali. You can't avoid them but you must steer away from them as best you can. When men are drunk, evil enters them and who knows what they will do?

His eyes are just tiny slits in his swollen face and he slurs his words as he looks at me. He looks like he's in his late forties. "Girl," he says, "you are toooo much beautiful."

My heart beats just a little bit faster.

"Thank you, Baba," I murmur, calling him "father" to emphasize his age, to remind him how young I am. Anyway, what does he care that I'm only fourteen? Lots of fourteen-year-old girls in Imbali go out with men his age. Even my friend Thandi dates older men.

Zi stands close behind me as I step up to the little window and ask the man for some bread, a box of milk, and Coca-Cola.

The man in the tuck shop looks me up and down. "He's right," he says. "You're becoming a beautiful young woman."

I know why they're noticing me. Lately my entire body is rebelling against clothes. I'm finally becoming a woman and it's obvious I'll be curvy, like Mama. If only I had Mama's small nose and big eyes! *Oh, Babamkhulu,* I think, *why was I born the same day you died? Couldn't you have waited and passed your spirit into one of your other descendants?*

I pass my money through the hole in the wire netting, taking my things and turning away.

"Why don't you sit with me for awhile? *Lapha!*" The drunk man pats a stone step next to his bucket. He tilts forward, expectant, and almost falls off.

"Gogo's expecting me home," I lie, juggling the milk, bread, and Coca-Cola in my arms. I glance down the empty street towards our house, calculating how long it will be before Gogo and Mama will be home. If he were so bold as to follow us, I'd still have to wait some few hours before they returned.

"Your grandmother will wait. I'm sure she is a patient woman."

"No, Gogo expects me home *now* now." I tilt my head at Zi. "Besides, she's only five. She can't walk home by herself."

"She can stay." He grins, showing off his front teeth, yellowed and bleeding at the gums. His dry mouth makes a soft sound, *pah pah*, as he smacks his lips together. "But it's you I want to know better."

"No no no, my friend, leave her alone," the tuck shop owner says. "She's just a child. Let her grow a bit more, eh, *Ndoda?*"

"What are you talking about?" He's so drunk, he can't even stop squinting as he looks at me, greed pooling in his dark eyes. "She's young and look at her—hey hey! So fat!" He leers at me. "She's probably a virgin."

These older men are always obsessed with virginity. A virgin can't spread the disease of these days. But a virgin isn't protected from HIV í she can get it from one of these old men, if they are already infected. That's why I'm always telling Thandi to be careful with the men she dates.

"Sis, man, you're pathetic," the tuck shop owner says, turning away and going back inside his house.

Left alone with the drunk man, I look up and down the street again. It's still quiet, but now one or two young men are loitering at the end of the street, smoking cigarettes and glancing our way. *They* will not offer to help. No.

"Come on, Zi, let's run." I grab her hand, peeking back at the man, and at the red bucket, tilted forward like it's about to topple. "Quick quick."

But the drunk man is fast, whipping his hand out, grasping my leg, pulling me toward him, whirling me around, his fingers streaking across my thighs, his swollen eyes bugging out as I fall towards him. The milk tumbles in the dust at his feet.

"Ouch!" I screech.

"Come on, girl, give me some sugar," he whispers, one hand gripping me, the other crawling up my leg, fingers like little spiders.

I try to wrench my leg free but he has a strong grip, that man, and even as I jerk away, he rears back and I stumble towards him. A flash of blue from his shirt as I crash beside him in the dirt. A sudden stinging pain as the ground peels away layers of skin. My lips kiss the earth and I roll away, scrambling through the dust, tasting rust, smelling the metallic scent of blood.

"Khosi!" Zi shrieks.

On my hands and knees, I look at the drunken man, my vision blurring. His features haze over until they resemble a crocodile's, with a long snout and big hungry teeth.

The crocodile opens its mouth, ready to swallow me.

"Hey, man! Leave her alone!"

I glance up and see Little Man Ncobo standing between me and my attacker. A flash and the crocodile is gone, the drunk man glaring at me through Little Man's legs. He creeps back to his bucket, spit and vomit drooling out of his mouth onto the dirt.

What just happened? Did I imagine that man turning into a crocodile?

I push myself off the ground and brush dirt off my skirt. My knee is bloody.

"Did he hurt you, Khosi?" Little Man asks, his voice low, like we're having a private conversation. I've known Little Man all my life and we're even in the same class at school. He's a scrawny guy, short and skinny, but for now, he's like some hero in the movies, rescuing me.

"I'm okay," I whisper, ignoring the throbbing in my knee and trying not to limp.

He smiles at me and I can't help smiling back, suddenly noticing that his lips are the same blue-black color as his skin. In fact, I'm seeing all sorts of things about Little Man that I never noticed before. Like the way he leans toward me as he talks, close, his arm almost touching mine.

We have such different color skin—he's so dark in comparison. Like my *babamkhulu*. Like my *baba*.

My skin prickles. How is it you can know somebody all your life and only start seeing them some few minutes ago?

"You're all covered in dirt," he says, reaching out and brushing my arm.

His fingers are so gentle as they graze against my skin. I quiver, my heart beating fast. I'm not sure if it's racing because of the drunk man or because of Little Man touching me. Maybe it's both.

"What about the milk, Khosi?" Zi worries.

"Forget about it." I feel bruised where each of the drunk man's fingers wrapped around my thigh.

"But we need it for Gogo's tea," she protests.

"I'll get it," Little Man says.

As he trots over to retrieve the box of milk, the drunk man begins to shout at me. "I'll be here when you change your mind, little girl," he yells. "I'll be your sugar daddy! I'll buy you whatever you want! See? I have so much money!"

He reaches into his pocket and silver coins slip from his fingers into the dirt. He begins to comb the dust, searching for them.

Zi laughs. "Oh, you have too much money!" she calls.

"Don't be rude, Zi. Just ignore him." Even as I chide her, I wish I had her courage. And she's only five!

The next time an older man attacks me like that, I promise myself, *I won't be so helpless. They'll know just who they're dealing with.*

But even as I make that promise, I wonder if I'll have the courage to keep it.

"Catch it if you can, Zi," Little Man calls, throwing the box of milk into her outstretched hands. "Good catch." He grins at her and she grins back.

"I'll walk you home, Khosi," he says.

"Thank you." I'm glad Gogo is at the funeral. I can hear her voice grumbling in my head if she saw me with Little Man: *You can't even walk home for some few minutes without meeting some boy? What am I going to do with you? Don't you become one of those bad girls, always chasing after men.*

"Hey, it is not a problem," he says, his arm stroking against mine for some few seconds. It makes me shiver. "Cold?"

I nod, even though it's not true, and keep my arm near his, hoping we'll accidentally touch again.

He glances at Zi, who's watching us, curious. "You feel warm to me," he whispers, so low she can't hear.

It suddenly feels like a dozen monkeys are dancing in my stomach.

That's when it hits me. I have a *mad* mad crush on Little Man.

All this warmth is leaking out like tears from my eyes as I smile at him. Maybe I'll regret it later, letting him see how much I like him, but I can't hide it just now.

CHAPTER FOUR

DREAMS

I try to forget about what happened with the old woman and the drunk man, focusing instead on Little Man, my rescuer. But that night, nightmares flood my mind.

The worst is the one that finally wakes me, sweating and shivering and hot-cold all at the same time.

I'm flying high above Imbali, looking down through the smog at dozens of zigzag streets, twisting here and there, house after house after house crowded together, stair-stepping their way up and down hills and all the way to the city of Pietermaritzburg. An ambulance flashes its lights as it speeds around bends in the roads, goes down a wrong street and hits a dead end, backs up and turns around to try again to get out of the maze that is Imbali.

And then I see her. A witch—*my* witch, the woman who lives at the top of the hill—as she sneaks through the winding streets, as she passes each sleeping house, observing them all briefly until she comes to ours. And then she stops, staring right at the bedroom window where I sleep with Mama.

Though she doesn't say a word, I know she's daring me to come out and challenge her. I can hear her cackly voice speaking in my head: *Hah! So! You think good always defeats evil, eh? Well, why don't we find out, Nomkhosi Zulu?*

Don't do it, I whisper, but my body ignores my brain. It gets out of bed even while I scold it, even as I shout *Stop*! It walks to the window, and there I am, looking outside, watching that witch walk around and around and around the perimeter of our house, digging small ditches, scattering a white powder on stones, placing the stones in the holes, re-filling each ditch with dirt, then stomping down until nobody can find the spot where she dug.

Muthi. She's scattering a potion around our house, one that will harm anybody who steps into our yard.

No no no! Stop. I try to speak the words out loud but my voice strangles against the muscles of my throat.

She pauses to look at the bedroom window again, spreads her lips into a thin grin, and provokes me with her wordless taunt. *What are you going to do about it? How are you going to protect your family from this* muthi?

What did I do to deserve this? I ask. *Why am I your target?*

She laughs. *You think you and your family are innocent? Ah, but there was an opening to evil. You invited me.*

I didn't invite you, I argue.

Somebody in your household did. And now I'm daring you to come outside and we'll see who's stronger. You or me. Hah!

Who invited evil into our lives? I can't imagine Mama or Gogo or Zi doing anything that would cause this attack. Did I do something? I think back back back, months back. Of course, there are always these things that we should do for the ancestors, to ensure their protection over us. My family is not as faithful as we should be. But surely, our omission isn't so big that it would open the door so a witch thinks she is perfectly welcome in our home.

Our eyes meet. My fear collides with her hatred, like two taxis in a car accident. I start to shake and shiver.

There's no way I'm going outside and facing her, alone.

And she knows it. She knows I'm a coward. That's why she laughs, her mouth open wide, gold glinting on her front tooth. She laughs and laughs and laughs. At me. But it's the strangest thing. *There's no sound anywhere*, like God opened my eyes and plugged my ears.

She puts her fingers in her mouth and whistles until a baboon lumbers over from the shadows and kneels. She climbs on and rides away, still laughing.

Mama shakes me awake. "Khosi," she's shouting, "*vuka*! Wake up!"

I'm standing next to the window, the same window in my dream.

"You must have been sleepwalking," Gogo says. She looks like she wants to ask more, but respects my privacy too much.

Zi isn't so respectful. She's sucking her thumb, the scarf we managed to tie on her head last night clinging to a single knotted plait. "Were you having a nightmare?"

"No!" I deny it quick quick. But I know this much: dreams don't come out of nowhere. They are signs, sent from the ancestors as warnings. They've bothered me for two nights in a row now. What *is* it they're trying to tell me?

I close the door to the toilet and sit on the edge of the bathtub, looking down at my feet, following the cracks in the linoleum from one end of the room to the other, trying to forget what I saw.

CHAPTER FIVE

Visit to the Sangoma

Gogo has trouble getting out of bed the next morning, sore from her walk up the hill to go to the neighbor's funeral.

"Why don't you stay in bed, Gogo?" I suggest. "God will understand if you miss church just once because you are so tired."

But no matter how tired she is, or how sick, Gogo always goes to church. "God never says, 'I'm too much tired, I don't think I'll forgive your sins today,'" she says now as she struggles to sit up.

I glance quickly down at her swollen knees. Gogo gasps as she tries to stand and I reach forward to give her support. We hobble into the dining room, where Gogo collapses on the sofa and Zi sits beside her, patting her arm. I pull a little table forward and lift Gogo's feet to help bring the circulation back.

"I'll go to the *sangoma* after church and get some *muthi* to bring the swelling down," I say. I need to see the *sangoma* myself—to talk to her about the dreams...about what happened yesterday...about the drunk man who looked like he turned into a crocodile...

Mama stands in the doorway of the kitchen. "She needs to go to the doctor, Khosi," she says.

"The *sangoma's* herbs always work, Mama." *Please, Mama, I need to go.*

"A doctor's medicine will work even better," Mama says.

"But when can she go to the doctor?" I ask. "She can't go alone and by the time I'm back from school, it's too late, the clinic is closed."

Mama closes her eyes at the impossibility of it all. She leaves early Monday morning and comes home late on Friday night. After helping MaDudu last week, she can't miss another day of work—we depend on her small salary for every last penny.

"I can stay home from school and take Gogo to the clinic this week," I offer, sinking inside.

Mama shakes her head. "School is too important."

Anyway, if I stay home from school, Zi has to stay home from school, too. She is too young to walk through Imbali by herself or to catch a taxi to go into the city, where we are lucky enough to go to a private school because we have scholarships.

"Then let me go to the *sangoma* and get some herbs. It's brought the swelling down in the past, Mama."

Mama sighs. "It's the best way. For now."

I sit down beside Gogo and put my arm around her. "There are people from the parish who will come and let you celebrate mass here at home," I say. "I'll ask them to come this afternoon. You stay here and rest. Next week you'll feel better."

So Gogo stays home from church, for the first time I can remember. While Mama is in the toilet getting ready, Gogo calls me to her side. I lean in close. "Don't forget, tell the *sangoma* about the witch," she whispers.

"That will be expensive, Gogo," I say.

She fiddles around in her pockets and hands me fifty *rand*. "If you can only pay for one thing, forget my *muthi*. It is not so important as blocking that old woman's evil."

Mama locks the gate behind us, and we start walking up the hill toward our church, the Catholic one, which is just behind the water tank covered in bright, bold graffiti. Zi dances ahead of us, calling hello to the people we pass.

We walk past house after house, past the tall buildings of flats, *tsotsis* hanging out on the top floors, smoking *dagga,* shaking their dreadlocks, and shouting insults at us.

"Yah, *Ntombi,*" they scream at me. "Come have a good time!"

Mama shakes her fist at them but they just laugh and stare at us. At me. "I don't like the way men are looking at you, Khosi," she says.

"I never come this way alone," I say. I've already learned to avoid the places where *tsotsis* hang out. I don't like the way they approach, slow, like they have all the time in the world. They pass by me, staring, their faces a mask but their eyes lit up with—with what? Something I don't want to see. I've never seen a *tsotsi* smile, though surely they must, somewhere, sometime...right? Maybe they smile at their mothers.

But Mama isn't done fretting. "No, you need to be very careful."

It's like Mama thinks I don't know what those men could do to me. I may be young but I have friends all over Imbali and they tell me just what happens if you flirt with danger. Even one of them, Sibu, told me it can happen with men you know. Her own uncle crawled into bed with her one night! She didn't dare tell her parents.

I'm glad my mother's brother Richard is nothing like that. When he comes home on the weekend—*hayibo!*—the only thing I have to worry about is his dirty socks. He has never tried what what what with me. No, he is just like Gogo and Mama, always telling me not to be like other young women. "*Wena uzihloniphe,*" they say, over and over. "Respect yourself. Protect your virtue." Though I agree with what they say, I don't understand how you are responsible for protecting your virtue if a man attacks and overpowers you.

"I don't need a bodyguard," I say, impatient.

But of course, Mama isn't comforted by my words. So I try again. "Mama, the farthest I go alone is to the *sangoma's* house to pick up herbs for Gogo. That's only some few streets away."

"I wish you didn't ever have to leave the house, *mntwana wam',*" she says finally, smiling.

"That is impossible," I say, treating her comment like a joke. But horror clamps around my heart. My world is small enough as it is—Gogo only lets me go from home to school, the tuck shop near our house, the vegetable market, or the *sangoma's*. If I am gone even some few minutes longer than she thinks I should be, she gets so worried. One time last year, I lost our taxi money. So after school, Zi and I had to walk from the city all the way back to Imbali. It took an hour. By the time we arrived, she was sending an entire *impi* of neighbors all over Imbali, looking for us.

Still, Gogo doesn't have a choice. She is too old to go with us everywhere and she depends on me to buy food and run other small errands while Mama is gone. Like Mama, my uncle Richard works far away, and he comes home even less often than she does.

"Mama, don't worry about Khosi," Zi says. She has stopped dancing around in front of us and is holding Mama's hand. "I'm *always* with her. I'll protect her. Just yesterday..."

I look at Zi and shake my head slightly. *Don't tell Mama about that man that grabbed my leg yesterday.*

But Mama's laughing. "You're right, Zi, why am I so worried? You'll take care of her." And she reaches out to smooth Zi's hair.

Families file inside the sanctuary and sit in the pews. Some women are dressed in our church uniform, a white and purple gown. They prance down the aisle, looking special, like they belong more than the rest of us who just sit here in our ordinary Sunday clothes. We can't afford the uniform. Some of these women can't afford it either, but they scraped and saved for weeks, maybe months, to buy it.

Mama starts singing beside me and I join in, Zi dancing and whirling beside us, as the priests walk down the aisle holding high the cross with the crucified Jesus Christ. *Alleluia. Alleluia. Amen.* We stand as they pass, make the sign of the cross, then sit when they reach the front of the sanctuary.

When I was younger, I used to have trouble putting together all the different things we believe. There's God, the ancestors, the saints, and Jesus. Who should I pray to?

"Pray to all of them," Gogo told me. "The spirits of the ancestors are like the saints. When we are in trouble, we can call on them. The Lord-of-the-Sky is in heaven but the departed are still here with us on earth."

"Why don't we just pray to the Lord-of-the-Sky?" I asked. "He's the most powerful."

"Sho!" she exclaimed. "God is too busy to be doing what what what every time we pray. With all the thousands of people praying all at the same time asking for *everything*, do you think that God can hear all of us at once? I do not think so. We worship God only but we are grateful for the people who can help us on earth. Your ancestors are the people who gave you *life*, Khosi. They will trouble you when you have misbehaved. They will help you when you do what's right."

Mama, Zi, and I stand as we join in collective prayer. I wonder if it makes a difference when thousands of us—millions even—are all praying to God for the same thing, all at once? Does he hear us then?

"For all those suffering from AIDS, tuberculosis, and cancer, we pray to the Lord," the priest says.

I peek around the congregation. Everybody here—*everybody*—has a relative who has died or is dying of AIDS. But we never talk about it. No. Not in public.

"Lord, hear our prayer," we murmur.

After church, my friend Thandi nearly knocks me down with her hug. "I have so much to tell you," she squeals.

Thandi always has so much to tell me, even though I saw her in school just two days ago. Thandi is not what Gogo would call a "good girl." She has had more boyfriends than I can remember, and most of them are sugar daddies, older men who buy her things. I think she has gone all the way with them, and she's my age! One of these days, she will fall pregnant. One of these days, she may get sick from what they give her. I hope not, but it is a common problem. Two of my uncles died from HIV already. How does anybody think they will be the lucky ones to be spared?

"You have a new boyfriend?" I guess. Thandi can meet a man on the short walk from the taxi stop to her house and by the time she's reached her front door, he's already proposed.

I'm not disappointed. She flips open her cell phone and shows me his picture. "He owns a jewelry shop downtown," she boasts, holding out her hand to show me the slender gold band on her right index finger. "He's already given me *so* much cellphone airtime, I can talk whenever I want."

"Thandi, he looks way too old for you," I say. Not that Thandi cares. She likes older men. *And* their money.

"He's not *that* old." Thandi frowns, grabbing the cell phone back. She inspects his picture.

"He has a beard," I point out. "And it's gray."

"I don't care. Girl, he has *so much* money."

This thing isn't worth the argument. "Anyway, is your grandmother working today?" Gogo and I like Thandi's grandmother because she is honest. Some *sangomas*, they are just trying to make money and what what what. But if Makhosi thinks you need to go to the doctor, or that she can't help you, she'll say so.

"Yo, she had such a long line waiting for her when we woke up this morning," Thandi says. "That is why she isn't in church."

"Can I walk home with you? I need to get some *muthi* for Gogo." I'm not about to tell Thandi about the witch.

"*Yebo*, let me tell Baba."

I don't want to be like Thandi, but I'm jealous of one thing: she lives with her father. I will never live with Baba. When I was Zi's age, I wished Mama and Baba would get married. I didn't understand then how expensive is this thing of *lobolo*. In order to marry my mother, my *baba* has to give Gogo a lot of money. Back when Gogo was a girl, men gave cows to the bride's family. These days, they just give money instead. But still, it's too expensive. That's why not many people get married.

Baba is one of those men who can't afford it. When he was a young man, younger even than me, he left school and joined the struggle against apartheid, training as a soldier in Mozambique. He came home after the government released Nelson Mandela and they started negotiating to become a democracy, so blacks could have the vote for the first time ever in our own country. But then he was too old to finish school and now he struggles to find a good job. Sometimes he works for a day here or a day there. But paying *lobolo* to marry Mama? It is *too much* money.

So Thandi is lucky, living with her *baba*, seeing him every day. I only see mine some few times a year.

Thandi runs off to find her father and I find Mama among all the people lingering at the door. She gives me permission to go. I watch as she and Zi begin the long walk down the hill, past all the tiny houses and the tall buildings, all the way to our little house, set on the edge of Imbali, where the houses bleed into Edendale, another township. There are so many of us, sometimes it seems like the houses go on and on forever, all the way across South Africa.

I sigh when I see the long queue stretching all the way from the round hut in the back to the neighbor's yard. Weekends are a popular time to visit the *sangoma*.

As I wait in the queue, I finger the fifty *rands* Gogo gave me to pay for the medicine, winding the paper around my index finger. Mama thinks *sangoma* medicine—honoring the ancestors—is silly, maybe even wrong, but here I am. And so are all these other people. Why? Because we know something Mama doesn't. She's the smartest woman I know... but she hasn't figured out that science doesn't explain *everything*.

When it's my turn to enter the round hut, I take off my shoes, smiling at the *sangoma's* apprentice. I wish I could help people the way she will when she's done with her training and working as a healer. But you don't choose to become a *sangoma* the way you choose to become a doctor or nurse; you're selected by the spirits of your ancestors. If they want you, they'll make your life miserable until you say yes.

She gestures for me to enter the hut. "*Ngena,*" she says.

I squat down on my haunches to crawl through the small hole near the ground.

The entire hut smells pungent, bittersweet like strong incense. A small fire smolders in the corner, belching short billows of smoke. The ceiling is black with burnt ash. Bunches of dried herbs and a beaded cow's tail hang from the ceiling, while an orange cloth sags across the wall. The floors are mud, smeared with cow dung in circular patterns.

There's a sound like the wind blowing through a field of tall grass. I look around, wondering where the noise is coming from, but there's nobody in the hut except for me and Thandi's grandmother, the *sangoma*, who's sitting in the central part of the round hut, her mouth closed.

"*Sawubona*, Gogo *ká*Thandi," I greet her, bowing low to the ancestral spirits inside her.

"*Yebo,*" she replies. Her long red beaded plaits clank as she nods her head at me.

As I tell her about Gogo and her sore knees, I peek at her wild outfit, wondering if it sometimes embarrasses Thandi to see her *gogo* dressed like this. Even though Makhosi is a modern *sangoma* and believes in doctors and nurses, she is still very traditional in the way she dresses and the way she approaches the ancestors. Everything she wears connects her to the spirit world and protects her from evil: the red and black beaded cap with a strip of cheetah fur threaded through it, the piece of blue cloth with pictures of spears and shields tied around her waist, the red ochre she rubs on her body until she shines a dull muddy red.

"I will give you the usual herbal remedy for sore knees," Makhosi says, reaching up to the ceiling and breaking off big handfuls of dried herbs. She shakes them together in a small gourd, rattling the herbs inside. She pours the mixture onto some newspaper, wraps it up, and hands it to me. "Steep it in boiling water. She must drink it three times a day until the swelling goes down."

When I take the folded up newspaper, her hand rests lightly on top of mine. "There's something else, is it, Khosi?" Makhosi and Gogo have been friends for many years. She feels like another grandmother to me. To know that she's on our side and we can always seek out her help...it means the world to me.

My throat is dry. The rustling sound becomes a low whistle.

"As soon as you walked inside this room, the spirits started shouting all at once," she says.

"Is that...is that the whistling sound?" I ask.

Her fingers tighten on my wrist. "You can hear it?"

"Only a little. What are they saying?"

"They're saying you're in danger, little Khosi. Tell me why. Do you know why?"

I swallow. "Do you know that old woman who lives in the two-story house at the top of the hill, near the water tank, just before you reach the Zionist church? The woman that everybody says turns people into zombies?"

She nods.

"Yesterday, when I walked Gogo to our neighbor's funeral, she spoke to me. She told me she's coming for me and nothing on earth can stop her.

She dug her fingernails into my arm." I hold out my forearm for Makhosi to show off the shallow gouge, already scabbing over. "Do you think...do you think she's cursed me? I had a terrible dream last night that she came and challenged me to a fight. I don't want to fight her!"

Makhosi reaches behind her and grabs a large stick of dried *impepho*. Lighting it, she waves the smoke in front of her nose, breathing in deeply, closing her eyes, and humming.

I start to speak again, but she holds up her hand to stop me.

At last, she opens her eyes. "It is almost true, what that old woman said," she says. "Almost."

"What part is true?"

"She is coming for you, that is true. And I cannot stop it. I do not know what is going to happen, Khosi. I can give you some *muthi*; I do not know if it will help. But my spirits are telling me that there is somebody who can stop her."

I hold my breath.

"They are saying it is you, Khosi. With the help of your ancestors, *you* can stop her."

Something claws and scrabbles inside of my stomach. "I'm like a rat which the cat plays with. How can I stop her? She's a witch!"

She folds her hands across her stomach. "You must remember to honor your ancestors every day, to make sure they are protecting you," she says. "Offer a little food and drink to them in the evenings and thank them for what they do for you. They will help you. That is what they are saying."

I stumble out of the hut, Gogo's *muthi* clutched tight in my hands. Perhaps the words Thandi's gogo spoke to me should fill me with confidence. But they don't. How could anybody think that I can stop a powerful witch? A witch with an army of zombies working for her?

CHAPTER SIX

Visiting Little Man

Instead of going straight home, I head towards Little Man's house, cutting through a corner alley behind Mama Thambo's *shebeen*. The blue light of the television spills out through the open door, where two men are lighting up and smoking *dagga*. The sweet odor drifts towards me. Inside, men and women are cheering for Bafana Bafana, South Africa's soccer team.

I wander past, ignoring the cat calls from the men standing outside. I'm deep in thought about what the *sangoma* told me. Usually, a visit to the *sangoma* is so comforting—either there's nothing wrong or she can help you fix it. But today...

When I look up, I can already see Little Man's yellow matchbox from a distance, crowded up against the houses next to it. His mother is growing a garden in the front yard; the corn looks like it's ready to harvest.

Despite the worry over the witch, my stomach clenches in excitement at the thought of seeing him. *I'll pass by slowly, just once,* I tell myself. *Maybe he'll be outside so I can say hi.*

Seeing Little Man will make me feel better, I realize, even as I think, *Gogo would* kill *me if she knew about this.*

When I reach Little Man's gate, his dogs run out, howling in greeting. The gate swings open and Little Man strolls out, whistling, winking at me like he knows I'm coming by to see him.

Anyway, I've gotten my wish and my heart leaps so far, it might as well have taken a fast airplane flight all the way to Zimbabwe.

While I'm trying to snatch it back from wherever it went, Little Man says, "Hey *wena* Khosi, what are you doing here?"

"I was just passing by," I gasp.

"Where were you going?"

Now I have to find an excuse. I never pass by his house except with my family on our way to church. "I was just at Thandi's," I say, pointing in the direction of her house. But of course, my house is in the wrong direction to come this way. *He's going to know I wandered by this way just to see him.* How embarrassing.

I'm getting hot and itchy. I'm hoping he'll ignore the fact that I wouldn't normally pass his house. I point to the wrapped newspaper full of Mama's *muthi*. "I'm just out getting some few small things for my *gogo*."

"That's cool," he says. "My *gogo* sends me to the *sangoma's* house to get *muthi,* too."

We're silent while I think of something to say. At school, my other friends help carry the conversation so there are no awkward silences.

I ask the first thing that comes to mind. "Have you ever gone to a *sangoma* when you were sick?"

He shakes his head no. His tightly coiled dreads reach to his shoulders and swing with the movement of his head. I like them. No, I *love* them.

"We go to the doctor if we're sick," he says. "That *sangoma* medicine, it's all superstition and lies."

All those warm fuzzy feelings I have for him dry up in defensiveness. I don't want to argue with him, but I can't keep my mouth shut. "These herbs really help my grandmother with her arthritis."

"I bet doctors have some medicine for your *gogo's* arthritis that will help her a lot more than a bunch of old herbs."

"But herbs are natural, not like the medicine you get from doctors," I protest.

"Do you really believe in all that ancestor stuff?" Little Man asks.

"You don't?"

He shrugs. "I don't know what I think."

"I believe in it." I lower my voice, as though Gogo and Mama are listening in, even though they're nowhere around. Since Mama doesn't believe in things like that and Gogo does, I can't talk about it without offending *somebody*.

"Really? Why?"

"I've seen some things. And at the end of the day, I couldn't explain them."

"Like what?" he asks.

I think about everything that has happened in the last two days— the witch who told me she was coming for me and nothing could stop her, the drunken man who changed into a crocodile and then back into a man right before my very eyes. Did I just dream his sudden transformation? And that's another thing—the dreams I've been having, dreams so real it feels like I exist in two worlds at the same time.

But I don't know how to tell these stories to anybody else without sounding crazy. So I just shake my head.

"I thought you loved science," Little Man says. "Aren't you making the highest marks in biology?"

I nod. "I think it's interesting to learn about the human body. I like learning about diseases and how people cure them."

I don't really know how to explain how I feel about biology—like I belong somehow. It's as if everything I learn, I already knew, somewhere deep inside, but biology gives me the words I need to talk about it. At the same time, I know there are things it can't explain about the human body. Maybe that should be a scary thing, but it's actually comforting. At the end of the day, we still need God.

"But you still believe in witches and ancestors? Scientists say those things don't exist. So if you love science, how can you believe in those things?"

"I just think there's a lot science can't explain," I say. "Maybe someday we'll understand how it all fits together, but as for now...no matter how much we know, it's still a mystery."

He swipes up my heart with his smile. "That's what I like about you, Khosi," he says. "You always say just what you think."

I *wish* that was true! Little Man sees me with different eyes than the ones I use to judge myself.

Little Man leans forward and whispers, like we're in some conspiracy, "Okay, if I was dying, I'd go to the *sangoma*. What would I have to lose? It might help and it won't hurt. My *gogo* swears by it and I *love* my *gogo*."

Somehow I don't think *my gogo* would like it if she knew a young man was grinning at me like this. But *I'm* so glad, I'm bursting. Maybe... maybe...maybe Little Man likes me, too.

"Have you ever heard the joke about the woman who went to see a *sangoma* because her daughter-in-law had cast an evil spell on her?" he asks.

"No."

"Yeah, the old lady had been cursed with so much toe jam, her feet were stinking like—*whew!*—a chicken's arse."

Now we're both laughing. But soon the laughter turns into what-do-I-say-next awkwardness.

Little Man kicks at the dust with his flip-flops.

"Are you watching the Bafana Bafana game?" I ask.

"Sis man, it's as if you think I'm not South African," he says. "Of course I'm watching! In fact, I'm missing the game because I came outside to talk to *you*."

When he says that, it feels like I'm dropping from the top of a tall building and falling fast towards concrete. I'm reluctant to leave but if he really wants to be watching the game instead... "I can't stay. I need to go home."

"I'll walk you," he says, quick quick, and my heart leaps again, hurtling forward, fast like a cheetah.

"Oh, I wouldn't want to keep you from watching the game," I say, wishing immediately that I hadn't opened my mouth. *Of course*, I want him to walk me home. I just don't want him to feel obligated.

"You live five minutes away," he says. "I won't miss much."

But there's a bigger problem. "Gogo might be angry if she sees me with a boy."

"I could put on my mother's skirt and we could pretend I'm a girl. But Mama's so much fatter than me, I don't think it would stay up." He grins at me. "I'd walk through the streets of Imbali, showing everybody my underwear."

I can't help laughing. Little Man is as skinny as a hyena. Who cares if a man is skinny? It's women that should be nice and fat in order to grow babies.

"Anyway, I'll see you in school on Monday," I say, smiling at him. "Bye, Little Man."

"Bye, Khosi," he says. He pauses for a second, and then adds, "It was really fun talking to you. Thanks for coming by."

I'm so happy to hear that! On the way home, I can't help it—I dance the *toyi-toyi*, shifting my weight from one foot to the other and shaking my fist in the air. When people see me, they wave their fists in response and call out, *"Amandla!* Power!"

"Awethu!" I wave back and *toyi-toyi*, winding my way through the maze of streets that make up Imbali.

The cell phone rings, interrupting my dance. It's Gogo, wondering where I am.

"I'm coming now now," I say, hanging up just as somebody grabs me from behind with the crook of his arm.

The cell phone flies through the air and lands in the dirt.

I start screaming.

"Shut up," the drunk man says, rough, choking me with one arm, forcing all sound back into my throat. He holds me firm against him, his body curving around mine, his fingers brushing against my neck, scaly and cold.

Crocodile skin.

God, please please help me.

I struggle against his arm, kicking at his leg—all the time, gulping at air, the way I imagine I would if I flew up, up, up, so high that oxygen disappears. Black light creeps up over my eyes, blocking the world out, but not before I see his face looming over me as I crash onto the packed dirt road.

CHAPTER SEVEN

MAMA'S GUMPTION

"This drunk man I saw sitting at the tuck shop the other day just attacked me," I tell Mama and Gogo. They are sitting in the kitchen, drinking tea, the door open to provide a breeze.

Mama inspects the red marks on my arms where he grabbed me. My head aches, but I don't know if it was the choking or falling that caused it. *He touched my neck.* The neck is the place of anger. If somebody touches you there, they want you to die. He is *that* angry with me. But why? What did I do to him, except refuse to let him be my sugar daddy?

I don't mention the way his skin felt, like crocodile skin—Mama would scoff at me if I said anything—but I wonder: Could he be a sorcerer? There's something evil about him. Something more than just a drunk man.

"Men!" Mama rages. "They think they can just get away with anything."

"But what are we going to do, Elizabeth?" Gogo rocks back and forth on her chair, one of the legs wobblier than the others. "There are drunk men everywhere."

"That is true. But *this* drunk man attacked our daughter."

"Do we know this man, Khosi?" Gogo asks. "Do we know his family?"

I shake my head. "But lately, he is always at the tuck shop around the corner."

"What is happening to us?" Gogo sips her tea and looks out the open door, her eyes distant, seeing nothing in front of her. "In the past, it was always the men who protected the community. And now, they are the ones we must fear."

She reaches out and grabs my hand, her eyes focusing on mine. "You must be careful, Khosi," she says. "Not just with this man, but with every man, especially if they are drunk."

I nod even though this is something I already know.

"I am not going to sit here and scold my girls to be more careful." All Mama's anger gives her sudden energy. "Come with me, Khosi! We're going to pay this little coward a visit."

She grabs my hand and, like two determined crazy women, we march out the door and down the street. Actually, Mama's the mad woman and I'm lagging behind, wishing I hadn't told her who attacked and robbed me.

"Don't go so fast, Mama." I hope maybe she'll turn around and we'll go back to the house and pretend this never happened.

She glances at me, quick quick, then turns back to the road. "Why didn't you fight him off?" Her voice, demanding.

"I tried." Now the tears are spilling down my face. Why is Mama blaming me for something I couldn't help? "He surprised me. I wasn't prepared."

"Izzit?" She slows down so that I'm beside her. She reaches out with a rough hand and wipes the tears from my face. It stings where she touches me. "You didn't try hard enough," she says.

"He was stronger than me," I protest. "He was choking me!" I point to the red marks on my neck, where he held me with the crook of his arm.

Now she gets up in my face, fierce and unrelenting. "And next time, he could rape you or kill you. Is that what you want?"

There's nothing to say. I can't tell Mama that he had animal strength. So I just look at the dirt, to avoid Mama's accusing gaze.

"You *must* learn to notice what's going on around you and defend yourself."

I open my mouth to protest, then remember how I *wasn't* noticing anything when he attacked me. I was just too happy about Little Man.

"Very soon, you are going to need more courage than ever before," she says. She reaches out again and wipes more tears from my face, her touch still harsh but this time, there's a gentleness behind it. "Don't *ever* let yourself be a victim, Khosi."

I wonder why Mama thinks I'm going to need courage? I'm too afraid to ask. And why is she blaming *me* for getting attacked? This is a new side to Mama.

The man is sitting on his bucket in front of the tuck shop, his eyes closed, his head nodding as he sleeps.

"Is that the man?" she asks me.

"Yes, Mama." I hope she doesn't make too much trouble for me. If she humiliates him publicly, what will he do to me the next time he catches me alone?

Mama snorts. "Him?" she asks again. "That tiny man?"

I nod, ashamed. He has surprising strength, I want to say, like a crocodile's.

Mama doesn't hesitate. She strides over, slapping him so hard, he falls off the bucket and lands in the dirt.

When he looks up, startled, Mama swoops down, grips his shirt, and shoves him back down.

Our eyes meet. His, coal-black and hard. *You'll regret this,* they say.

"Shame on you," Mama screams.

His eyes dart around, looking for something. A weapon, perhaps? An escape? He grips the earth, his fingertips curling around a clod of dirt.

Mama's firm hand presses him down. "Are you such a big man, to go around preying on young girls? Do you think you're so tough?" she yells.

The old man flicks his gaze toward me. "Is she your little protector?" he asks, contemptuous, like I'm Zi's age and need an adult to fight my battles.

I guess he's right. He knows he can't say a thing to Mama, so he goes for the weak one here—me.

"Khosi doesn't need my protection," Mama says. She lets go of him and wipes her hand on her skirt, as if his shirt made her hand dirty. "People will be watching you now. You won't bother her again."

Maybe Mama's certain of that, but when she turns her head to look at the small crowd that's gathered to watch this crazy woman beat up a man, he winks at me.

I suck in my breath. I knew it. I *knew* this could create trouble for me. Mama's gone all week long, and that's when I will have to face this man.

"If I hear you've done anything to her—" Mama shakes her finger at him and gestures at me to leave. "Believe me, you will wish you hadn't."

I *wish* that made me feel safe. But it doesn't.

As we walk away, I sneak a look backwards. The drunk man is just sitting on his bucket, laughing silently. At me.

If I were as strong and brave as my mother, he'd leave me alone. But I'm not. Even as Mama says, "He'll leave you alone now, Khosi," fear splits my heart right down the middle.

CHAPTER EIGHT

THE LIGHTNING BIRD

I tell Gogo all about the *sangoma* visit as we take Mama's freshly washed clothes off the line in the backyard. The air is growing hot and heavy with rain that wants to fall but doesn't.

"Khosi, why does it rain?" Zi asks, interrupting my conversation with Gogo. She's tracing the cracks in the cement with her fingers.

"You see, the sky is a man," I say. "And the earth is a woman. When it rains, he's sending his seed to the earth, so the earth can give birth to all the plants that feed us."

"So the sky and the earth are married?" Zi screws up her face at me.

I laugh with her. "Yes. And when the sky is angry with his wife for something she said, he punishes her by withholding his seed. And then the earth grows cracked and dry and infertile and pleads with her husband, 'I am a foolish woman, with a terrible temper. Please forgive me and send rain so I can be fertile and beautiful once again.'"

We hear the distant rumbles of thunder. It worries me. We never have lightning storms this time of year.

"And thunder?" Zi asks. "Why does it thunder?"

"Even God above has this thing of anger," Gogo says as we hurry inside with the last basket of clothes.

Auntie Phumzile and her girls arrive just as I fold the last skirt. "You're lucky we finished so you don't have to help," I tell my cousin Beauty.

Mama comes out of the bedroom and everybody crowds into the dining room. Beauty and I go into the kitchen to cook *phuthu* and beef—a treat that Auntie has brought—and Beauty tells me all the secrets she's saved up since last week.

"I have a boyfriend," she giggles.

"Izzit?" It seems sometimes that the whole world has a boyfriend, except *me*. I just want one, that's all. "Does Auntie know?"

The look she gives me makes me feel stupid. Of course, Auntie's just as ignorant about Beauty's boyfriend as Mama is about Little Man.

"I like someone too," I confide, looking at the carrots I'm chopping instead of looking at Beauty.

"Does he know you like him?" Beauty asks

"He must," I say. "I don't think I hide it very well."

"Shame. You shouldn't let a man know you like him, not until he asks you out." When Beauty shakes her head at me, her long lovely plaits linger on her shoulders, caressing her before they tumble down her back.

My own hair is just little tufts of curls sprouting all over my head like new plants shooting up through soil. We have the extensions, but nobody has time to plait my hair.

"Beauty, will you plait my hair today?" I ask. Maybe Little Man will notice if I come to school tomorrow with a new weave. Hair is important to him—it's taken him four years to grow his dreads.

"Of course," she says. Then she adds, as if she knows so much more than I do, "Men really like it when you have plaits in your hair. You watch, Khosi, this boy you like will tell you just what he thinks when you come to school tomorrow."

"I hope so."

After we eat, we crowd into the sitting room watching *Generations*, our favorite soapie. I sit on a chair and Beauty begins to work on my hair, tugging and pulling at each tuft to add the extensions. My scalp is already beginning to itch and she hasn't even finished yet.

Halfway through *Generations*, the electric storm begins. First the TV crackles and the picture dies. Then the entire room lights up in black and white contrast, so that when I look at the faces of my family sitting opposite me, they are pale, pasty white, like they no longer belong to the living.

Zi squeals and runs to hide in the bedroom. The two younger girls,

Beauty's little sisters, join her. Gogo's hands tremble as she totters to the back room, where the three girls are huddled together under the covers, on the bed Zi shares with Gogo. I used to do the same thing when I was Zi's age.

"What is this, a freak lightning storm?" Mama asks.

"I don't think it's safe for you to leave just yet," she tells Auntie.

"No, I'll wait until this passes," Auntie answers.

Mama steps over to the door and opens it. "Khosi." She gestures for me to join her. "Come watch this thing, God having a temper tantrum."

Because it's Mama, I swallow my fear. We stand together, watching as lightning strikes the ground like the tongue of an angry woman.

"Even though it's dangerous, there's something beautiful about it," I say. Even the fact that a witch can control lightning, using it to kill somebody, doesn't change how beautiful it is, the way it lights up the whole world in a sea of black and white light.

"It's like the ocean," Mama agrees. "Powerful."

I shiver. Mama puts her arm around my shoulder.

Auntie's voice echoes from the back bedroom, where she's busy chiding the little girls. "How can you be frightened by such a little thing as this? A lightning storm? And Mama, you should be ashamed, encouraging it!"

"She sounds just like you, Mama," I say.

"Neither one of us wants our daughters to be crippled by superstition."

"Do you really think Gogo is so superstitious?" I ask, knowing what her answer will be, wondering what she would think if she knew that, every night, I leave food and drink out for the ancestors.

This is what *I* think: Both Gogo and Mama are right, and they're also both wrong. Science is important. So are the old ways. We can explain some things through science but not *everything*. But because Gogo and Mama are so stubborn, it makes it really difficult to navigate a path between them, to be my own person, to assert myself. I don't want to offend either one of them. No, I want them both to be pleased with the person I become. That's the difficulty of my life.

But Mama surprises me. "Sometimes, even I believe things that aren't true." She laughs a little. "So perhaps I shouldn't judge your grandmother so harshly. Everybody has their own little superstition, heh, Khosi?"

It's not exactly a concession, but it's more than she's ever offered before.

We turn back to the open door, watching the play of light and dark dancing along the horizon.

It's so rare that we can be together like this, Mama and me. I stand there as long as she does, watching the sky light up with blue and white streaks of light before we close the door, then turn back to Beauty, who's waiting to finish plaiting my hair.

In my dreams that night, a bolt of lightning creeps into the house, sneaking in through the crack in the door. It knows my name, spoken by the witch. It skulks down the hallway, feeling from side to side, searching...searching... searching for me.

I wake up, bathed in sweat and unable to fall back to sleep. So I get up early to fix Mama a good breakfast before she leaves for Greytown.

While Mama bathes, I cook eggs and toast bread, placing them under a plate to keep warm. I even fry a small piece of fish I saved just for her sending-away breakfast.

But when I open the back door to empty the rubbish bin, there's a sudden fluttering of black wings, gigantic wings, wings as tall as I am. A man-sized bird. The wings flutter and flash, silver like lightning, quickly disappearing around the corner.

I run around the house, flinging rubbish to the side in my haste, but the bird is long gone, leaving only a streak of something like smoke lingering in the air.

It's nothing. That's what I tell myself as I pick up rubbish and place it back in the bin. *It's nothing.* At least, that's what Mama would say. She would laugh. "Sho, it is just a bird, Khosi. You're scared of a little thing like that? A bird?"

And I would have to admit, "It wasn't just any old bird. It was the *impundulu.*" I'd feel stupid telling Mama that. She'd insist it couldn't be true. I can hear her already, in my head. "Khosi, really! There's no such thing as a lightning bird. It's just something old people talk about. A folk tale, nothing more."

And what would she say if I persisted and said, "But what if that's what I saw, Mama? What if a witch put a curse on one of us and that bird is the sign?"

"Na! and who would want to harm us, Khosi? What have we ever done to create enemies?" That's what she would say, adding, "Even if people try to do something against you, the only power they have over you is your fear."

I've heard her say something like that many times.

So I keep telling myself, *It's nothing, just like Mama would say. It's just my imagination.* It's nothing except...it's not just the lightning bird. It's my dreams. And it's the witch—her threat, and the fact that she must have gotten some of my skin under her fingernails so she could send the *impundulu* to come for me, to kidnap or to kill me.

Still, I don't tell Mama when she joins me for breakfast. Or Gogo when she wakes up. I keep the lightning bird a secret.

Why? Because I hope I'm right. I hope it's nothing.

When Mama leaves, even though it's still dark, only 4 o'clock in the morning, our neighbor lady is waiting outside. Why isn't she inside, drinking tea and having breakfast? Or sleeping? What is she doing outside, staring at our house as if she wishes evil on us?

Though Mama greets her pleasantly, "Good morning, Mama..." MaDudu says nothing in response. She just shakes her fist at Mama's back when she steps outside the gate.

"Why did she do that?" I ask.

"She got angry when I told her there was very little money in her husband's insurance settlement," Mama says. She sighs. "Perhaps she is blaming me instead of her husband."

When I go back inside, I peek over at MaDudu's house. She is standing just inside, the door cracked open, watching as Mama walks down the road to the taxi stop.

PART TWO

THE CROCODILE

CHAPTER NINE

GROWN-UP GIRL

After Mama leaves, she stays in Greytown for too many weeks. She says she's just too busy to come home, but she used to come home every weekend, no matter how much work she had.

Zi misses Mama so much. Because she won't let anybody but Mama touch her hair, it starts to look ratty. I beg her, "Please, Zi, please let me comb your hair."

"No," she yells and runs under the bed to hide.

"Maybe we should shave her head," I suggest.

"Elizabeth will return soon, I'm sure," Gogo replies.

"Maybe Mama can talk to MaDudu when she returns," I say. Ever since Mama left, MaDudu has spent a lot of time in her yard, brooding over her broom and staring at our house. She won't speak to us about it, though. In fact, she isn't speaking to us at all, even when we greet her.

Gogo's face crinkles up in worry as soon as I mention the next-door neighbor. She's so short and small, it makes me want to protect her. "I don't know what is her problem."

Anger like MaDudu's is always something to fear. When people get too angry, who knows what they're willing to do, even to go so far as to make a bargain with the devil.

"I am sure MaDudu will forget about it just now," I say. But I don't think I reassure either of us. So I try joking: "It's just that the *tokoloshe* has been whispering lies in her ear all night long."

Zi's head pops out from under the bed. "What's the *tokoloshe?*" she asks.

Gogo and I look at each other. "You mean I haven't told you any tales of the *tokoloshe?*" Gogo says. "I will have to fix that at bedtime some night."

"The *tokoloshe* is a tiny tiny man," I tell her. "So tiny, he fits in the palm of your hand. He's hairy all over and he looks like he's half-baboon, half-man. He can turn himself into any shape he wants, though, and he's very mischievous. He likes to play mean jokes on humans."

"Have you seen the *tokoloshe?*" Zi asks.

"Once, when I was very young, I saw the *tokoloshe,*" Gogo says. "The missionaries in my village went to England and when they returned, they brought a ball for the children to play games. I was playing with a friend and she kicked the ball into the grass. I walked out into the tall grass, looking for that ball, and I couldn't find it anywhere! I walked as far as the grass went until I reached a pond. At last, I found it in the water. I started to pick it up and that's when I saw...*the ball had eyes.*"

"Wow," Zi breathes.

"What did you do?" I ask.

"I screamed and ran away. I knew it was the *tokoloshe* because we had *just* been talking about him. And I never did find the ball in the tall grass. Mr. Johnson, the missionary, was very angry with me that I had lost it. I did some work for him to pay for it."

"What about you, Khosi?" Zi asks.

"I've never seen the *tokoloshe,*" I say, "but my friends Thandi and Sibu were talking about the *tokoloshe* at school one day when, out of nowhere, came flying a note tied to an arrow. They read the note, and you want to know what it said?"

Zi nods. Then she shakes her head no. Then she nods again. Her eyes are wide.

I drop my voice to a whisper. "It said, '*Stop talking about me.*'"

Zi squeals and scrambles under the bed again.

"Oh, Zi," I say. "Don't be frightened. You can come out."

"The *tokoloshe* isn't going to hurt you," Gogo wheedles.

"It might play mean tricks on me," Zi says, her voice muffled.

"The *tokoloshe* only plays mean tricks on older people," I say. "Teenagers and adults."

"*Unamanga*," she says.

"It is not polite to tell somebody they are lying, Zinhle Zulu," I tell her in exasperation, getting down on my knees, trying to coax her to come out. But Zi won't move. I go into the kitchen to cook supper and, finally, when she's hungry, she creeps out and asks for something to eat.

One night, something happens that makes all of us forget about missing Mama. As I'm getting ready for bed, I notice blood on my underpants. "Gogo! Gogo!" I shout, both scared and excited all at once, the way you feel on the first day of school, the way I feel when Little Man grins at me and I wonder, *Does he like me, too?*

All the other girls at school—well, *Thandi*—started bleeding years ago. I'm so old, fourteen already, and I've been waiting and waiting, wondering if it would *ever* happen. I was even starting to get worried, so much that Gogo had started to talk about going to the *sangoma* to see if something was blocking the blood.

Still, Gogo doesn't share my excitement. She shakes her head and instant tears roll down her wrinkled black cheeks. "I'm not ready for you to grow up," she says.

Gogo cries so easily. Sometimes, it frustrates me.

"Nothing's going to change," I reassure her, even though we both know my words are meaningless. I'm an *intombi* now—a young woman, old enough to get married and have children. Everything will be different after this. *Everything!*

In fact, Zi's the one who says it. "Are you going to get a boyfriend now?" she asks.

Gogo must see the excitement in my eyes. "The tree is bent while it is young," she says. "Once a tree has grown, you can't change it."

"Gogo, I'm not a child anymore," I say. "My tree is already straight and tall."

Gogo laughs, but she looks sad. "Don't be so anxious to grow up, Khosi. There is still so much for you to learn."

"I guess I won't be running out and getting a boyfriend tomorrow then," I tell Zi and we both giggle.

"No, you better not," Gogo agrees, "or your mama will hide you away in some convent."

The next morning, all my excitement ebbs away when I get dressed in my school uniform. A green and white checkered skirt, a white button up shirt, a green vest, and long green knee-high socks. How could anybody feel grown up when they have to put these things on every day?

I don't look like an *intombi*. I look just like Zi. A little girl. How depressing. Even though he said he liked my new weave, is that what Little Man sees when he looks at me?

Gogo stands in the doorway of the bedroom, watching as we get dressed. "You're both growing up so fast," she sighs. "But when I look at you, I still see the moment you were born."

"What was I like as a baby, Gogo?" Zi asks.

"Sho! you came out squalling and red-faced, Zinhle. Right from the moment you were born, you demanded everything. I knew then you'd make your way in the world."

"And Khosi?" she asks.

"Eh-heh, Khosi, *her* birth was very strange." Gogo sits on the bed and adjusts her headscarf, her voice changing to her storyteller voice, the one she uses when she's telling us a folktale or describing what life was like in the old days, during apartheid. "Khosi didn't cry at all, not a single noise, not like any baby I've ever seen born before. It took you several days to find your voice. Even then, I told Elizabeth you had left your voice with the ancestors so you could be a voice from *that* world in *this* one."

I open my mouth to respond but no sound comes out. Why hasn't she ever told me this part of the story before? Something about the way she says it stirs a well of excitement deep inside me. I don't know what to do so I just let the giddiness spill out into a joke. "Next thing you know, Gogo, you'll say I should become a *sangoma*."

"Maybe you should," she answers seriously. "I am sure Babamkhulu must watch out for you in a special way."

Like Mama would ever let me study to be a *sangoma*! Anyway, I only wish I had the wisdom of the old ones locked up inside me. Even at school, my marks aren't as high as they should be—except in science. That's the one subject I really love.

I'm that glad I can tell Thandi I'm an *intombi* now, but I should have predicted her response. "Now you can get your own sugar daddy!" she says.

"Ew! I don't want an old man thinking he can touch me just because he buys me things."

"It's not like that," she says. "Kissing's nice. You'll see just how nice it can be."

"Not with an old man, it's not," I say. "Besides, you know what kissing leads to."

"Trouble," she giggles, agreeing.

Then she brings up a new subject. "Little Man's brother passed matric last year and graduated. He just found a job. They're slaughtering a goat to thank the ancestors for his good luck and everybody is invited to their house for a big party next month. Are you coming?"

"Mama won't let me," I say.

"You *have* to come," she insists. "Little Man said he *really* wants you to be there."

"Izzit?" Maybe I'm not like other girls but I think in this day and age, it's safer to like someone my own age. And maybe he didn't really say that, but I'm that hungry to believe her, a chicken pecking in the dirt for invisible seeds. So finally I say, "Okay, okay, I'll come. But what will I tell my mother?"

"Just tell her you're coming to my house to study," Thandi says.

Something twists deep in my stomach. "I've never lied to her before."

Thandi shrugs it off. "You'll have so much fun, you won't care. I'm telling you, we'll be the V.I.P.s of the party. There will be so many good-looking guys there."

I'm only interested in one good-looking guy, I think.

"It's nice to be young and pretty," Thandi continues. "You'll see. You'll meet so many men, you'll decide you don't need Little Man anymore."

"*Hayibo*, men? What will I do with a *man*, Thandi? Maybe I should just stay home. I'm not ready for this." Now I'm teasing her. I've already made up my mind to go. The last thing I want is for Little Man to meet someone else because I stayed home.

"Relax, *Ntombazana*," she says. "If you like little boys, Little Man will be there."

Ntombazana. Little girl. Baba calls me that, too. With Baba, it's a pet name. With Thandi, it's an insult. But maybe she's right. I certainly don't feel ready to entertain older men. I just like a boy my own age, that's all.

If that makes me a little girl, I can live with that.

CHAPTER TEN

BABA'S GIRL

My father calls some few days later. Even though Baba lives in Durban, just an hour away, we only see him some few times a year. It's too expensive to travel back and forth all the time. So instead, we try to talk on the phone often.

"Sawubona, Baba!" Zi screams into the phone. She garbles a story about why mosquitoes scream in people's ears. I think it's from a book her teacher read to the class. She's quiet while Baba talks on the other end.

"Khosi!" he says when she hands the phone to me. "Your mama told me how fast you're growing up, so I thought I must call to find out just how grown up my little girl has become."

So Mama must have told him I've become an *intombi* now.

"She's worried because I'm a *beautiful* young woman," I joke. "She gets sick just *thinking* about it."

"*Hawu!*" he chuckles. "Does she think you're going to be wild, like she was? Does she think you're going to start running around all over the place?"

"Was Mama wild when she was my age?"

"Sho, was she ever! She was like a lion, either sleeping or on the hunt."

"What, did she have a lot of boyfriends?" I ask.

"Don't go getting any ideas in your head, just because I told you how wild Mama was when she was young," he says. "Anyway, I wasn't talking about boys. I meant she was always getting into trouble because of her strong political ideas."

I like hearing about the days when Mama and Baba were young. Mama and Baba are older than a lot of my friends' parents. They are old enough that they participated in the liberation struggle.

Everybody was so fearless in the fight for our freedom! Children boycotted school and teenagers like my *baba* joined the guerilla soldiers. Men and women stopped paying rent on their government-owned houses. People like Mama marched in the streets to protest the government policies. They did all this so we blacks could be free, so that we would have the right to vote, so that we would have the same opportunities as whites.

"I wish I did exciting things like you and Mama did when you were young," I say. When I think about what people like Baba and Mama did for us, it makes me long for a different life, like there's something I should be doing, that I'm *called* to do, to make South Africa a better place. But whatever it is, I can't figure it out.

"Don't long for the old days," he says. "When your mama and I were young, we thought only about freedom. We sacrificed everything to fight for it. But now, without an education, I can't even find a decent job. I try and try, Khosi. Every day, I go knocking on doors and nothing. But *you* can go to school and really become something."

"I just feel so anxious," I admit. This is something I can't say to Mama or Gogo. They depend on me too much. "I feel like there are so many things I should be doing to help people but I don't know where to begin."

"*Ntombazana*, I felt the same way when I was fourteen," he says. "My grandmother used to say that each generation has its own challenges, its own work to do. You'll figure it out. Just give it time."

"Baba, I'm not a little girl anymore," I say. "I'm growing up and I'm going to do great things someday."

He laughs. "I'll always be proud of the fact that I struggled for our liberation, Nomkhosi," he says. "We did an important work. But let me tell you something. I wish we could have lived a normal life and gone to school." He pauses, then says, "Please just agree to be my little girl for a little while longer."

The truth is, I will always be his little girl, no matter what happens in my life or how "grown-up" I become.

"And," he continues, "you make sure you stay away from all those young men your mama is so worried about."

"But some boys are nice." I have to speak up for Little Man.

"Which one of them is so nice? Does this 'someone nice' have a name?" He becomes suddenly demanding.

"Baba, don't be so suspicious. I'm too young for all that."

"Not young enough," he emphasizes. "You see, you'll make me sick with worrying, just like you've done to your mama."

"And Gogo, too," I add, laughing with him. "That's why she goes to the *sangoma's* to get *muthi* for her arthritis. Her bones ache because I'm sooooo beautiful."

We're both laughing as we hang up.

CHAPTER ELEVEN

Thandi's Sugar Daddy

Thandi's jewelry-store sugar daddy disappears quickly, a week or two later. And almost as quickly, she finds a new boyfriend.

She tells me all about him while we walk from history class to our lockers to pick up our things and go home.

"His name is Honest, he drives a taxi, he says sometimes he can take the taxi out after work and pick me up. I can sneak out and we'll go dancing." She says this all in a rush. "He gave me this"—she holds up her wrist to show off the slender black-and-silver-beaded bracelet on her wrist—"and this"—she tilts her ears to show off the red, gold, and green beaded earrings dangling from her earlobes—"and those are just the first of many gifts, Khosi!"

"What are your parents going to say if they see these gifts men are giving you?" I shift my books, scouring the hallways, hoping to see Little Man.

"I'll sneak them in and out of the house."

"How old is this Honest?" I hope he's younger than the jewelry store owner, who looked like he was fifty years old. Or older.

"Thirty-three," she says.

"Thandi! *Thirty-three?* What's wrong with the boys our own age?"

"We can never be with men our own age," Thandi says. "Not with this problem of *lobola*. Older men are the only ones who can afford to pay *lobolo* to our parents, so they're the only ones getting married."

Lobola was always expensive, even in the best of times. Back when my grandmother was young, men were supposed to give eleven cows to a young woman's parents in order to marry her. Eleven cows! Of course, not everyone could afford that.

But you read in the papers that some parents today charge up to 50,000 *rands* for their daughter. What young man has 50,000 *rands*? A rich black lawyer, maybe. We're never going to meet men like *that* in the townships.

"I don't want to marry an old man just because he's the only one who can afford to pay *lobolo*," I say. "These days, you can get married without it."

It's true, some young people have given *lobolo* up because it's too expensive. I'm sure their parents are angry, losing all that money for their daughter, but we live in modern times. Mama would say it's time men stopped buying their wives, even while Gogo would protest and say that paying *lobolo* isn't buying a wife, it's linking two families together. I've heard them arguing about it. Gogo chides Mama for having two children with a man and never marrying him. "At least a man has never *owned* me," Mama always says, ending the argument.

Thandi laughs at my comment. "You think my *gogo* is going to let me get married without *lobolo*? You're really crazy, Khosi. In *my* household, *we* follow every Zulu tradition."

Baba is a very traditional man, just like Thandi's grandmother. He'll insist on *lobolo* when I get married too. And I *will* get married. I'll live with one man, and he'll be faithful to me, and we'll both avoid the three-letter plague—HIV—that's running around killing everybody in our country. These days, getting married is more important than ever, but it better have nothing to do with a man owning me. Because if it came down to *that*, I agree with Mama one hundred percent.

"Okay," I say, "but that doesn't mean you have to run around with older men. In a few years, maybe you can find a young man you like, and he can pay *lobolo* through an installment plan."

Thandi laughs at me.

"What? Why are you laughing? A lot of men are doing that these days."

"You think I want to wait ten years to get married because it takes him that long to pay?" she asks. "No thanks! I'd be an old woman marrying an old man. I'm telling you, Khosi, the only solution is to get yourself a sugar daddy."

Just then, we spot Little Man playing around with Victory Shabangu at the other end of the hall. When he looks up, I wave. But Victory whispers something to him, and instead of waving back, he turns his back. He and Victory keep fooling around, slamming locker doors.

My stomach clenches. "Are you sure Little Man said he wanted me to come to his brother's party?" I ask.

Thandi laughs. "You should give up your obsession," she advises. "Older men know how to treat a woman. They wouldn't ignore you like he did just now."

My stomach cramps and a searing fear runs through my entire body.

"Little Man's my friend," I say, still feeling the sting. That sting quickly changes to anger. With Thandi. "Besides, how do you know your older man isn't already married?"

"Thanks, Khosi!" she shouts, offended. "You're just jealous."

It's true. I spoke in anger, but there's more to it than that. There's a voice inside my head, telling me that there's something ugly in her future. "How do you know this Honest is somebody you can trust?"

She looks wounded by my question. "Khosi, what you don't understand is that all men like sugar on the side," she says. "It's just what our men do. Even my *baba* has a girlfriend. I bet *your baba* has another girlfriend besides your Mama, maybe he even has other children—"

"Shut up, Thandi," I interrupt her, to stop the flow of words streaming out of her mouth. It isn't something I want to think about, Baba putting Mama in danger like that. "If Honest has a girlfriend on the side, you should be careful."

"Careful?" she asks.

Why is she pretending? "Don't close your eyes, Thandi," I say. "You see the billboards. You see the ads on TV. You know about HIV, how it spreads."

She shrugs. "I like the gifts Honest gives me."

"I don't need gifts." For sure, I don't need the big gift that sugar daddies leave their girlfriends, the big gift that causes them to lose weight, get sick, and die.

But then Thandi looks shy as she says, "And he makes me feel beautiful."

"Good," I say. "That makes me happy." I'm not lying. Even if what I see in her future scares me.

CHAPTER TWELVE

MARKED

I don't like to talk about the dreams but they are always there, invading my sleep and waking me with the feeling that somehow I'm living a double life. The fourth or fifth time I wake screaming, Gogo sends me to the *sangoma* for some herbs.

"You are too much worried," she says. "What is this thing, bothering you? Is it that witch?"

"*Angaz'*," I say. I don't want to tell her what happens to me in my dreams. If I say it out loud, it might happen in real life.

So after school one day, Zi and I walk to Thandi's house with her. I have fifty rand in my pocket and a request for herbs to stop the nightmares. Zi waits outside the hut, talking to the *sangoma's* apprentice while I go inside.

While we talk, Makhosi spreads newspaper on the floor. She mixes herbs together with her long fingernails, then pours the herbs into small glass jars.

She shakes her head when I tell her about all the dreams bothering me. "I do not want to give you something to stop the dreams," she says. "The ancestors are sending them, trying to help you."

"How do you know it's the ancestors?" I guess I already know it's the ancestors—the dreams are always white, and that is their trademark—but I want her to confirm it.

"It is their way," she says. "It is how they communicate with those people they have decided are worth bothering, people who will listen, people like you, Khosi."

"Are you troubled by dreams also?" I ask, watching the pattern she creates in the herbs as she mixes.

"Sho!" she says. "It is terrible! When you become a *sangoma*, the ancestors never let you rest. They fill your sleep with other people and spirits and recipes for new *muthi* to cure this or that illness. It is *too much* difficult." She smiles at me. "You go to sleep, never knowing if that is the night they will get you up out of your warm bed and say, 'No, you mustn't sleep. Go here, do this.' You wake up in the morning, not knowing where you will go that day or what you will do. Even if you had planned to spend the day with your family, you must obey."

At least she is never in doubt what she must do: obey her spirits. I am all the time torn between Mama and Gogo, the new world and the old world, the science I learn at school and the African medicine Gogo sends me to fetch.

Before I leave, she hands me a small wrapped newspaper with herbs. "Take this," she says. "Perhaps it will help the ancestors clearly mark the path you should take in your dreams."

At home, I stir the herbs into a big pot of hot water and drink it all after eating, just like Makhosi prescribed. Then I join Gogo and Zi in the dining room.

I have homework I must do but I can't concentrate. Even when I try to watch television, my eyes keep focusing on the picture of Babamkhulu that rests on the mantle just above the TV.

He looks like he wants to say something to me. His stern expression is morphing as he furrows his brow and gazes at the three of us, his lips puckered up, mouthing words I can't hear.

I glance from the picture of Babamkhulu to Gogo and Zi. They are watching TV and don't seem to notice Babamkhulu's mouth moving.

My head starts to ache as his face blurs into fast movement, the worry spilling over into rapid head movements, his mouth open so wide, it looks like he's shouting at me.

Nausea spills over me in waves as my head spins.

"I'm going to bed," I mumble, stumbling off the sofa and going down on all fours, like an animal, rocking back and forth. The floor won't stay still. It's rolling like a river of water speeding downhill on the way from its source to the ocean.

I crawl across the floor, looking for places that are steady and reliable, but it heaves and buckles wherever I rest my hand. I sit back on my haunches, contemplating how I'm going to get to the bedroom.

My body feels heavy, as though it's going to sink right through the floor and drown somewhere beneath the earth.

"Khosi, what's wrong?" Gogo calls from what seems an ocean's distance away. Then she's beside me, reaching out her hand through the watery waves.

"I don't feel well," I mumble, grasping her hand, letting her help me stumble into bed.

Zi and Gogo stand over me, the same worried expression on their faces. "Do you want some food?" Gogo asks.

"No," I say. "I just want to sleep."

She covers me with a blanket.

"Do you want some water?" Zi asks.

"No. Leave me alone."

Closing my eyes only makes the spinning worse. So I stare at the ceiling, which is no longer the ceiling but the road outside our house, the one that leads to the tuck shop and that drunk man, who is sitting on his bucket, drunk, nodding off.

As I float past, his hand snakes out, fast, grips my shirt and pulls me towards him, so close I'm looking at the tiny yellow lines streaking across the whites of his eyeballs.

"Who's going to save you now, *Ntombi*?" he growls, shaking me so hard, I can feel my bones move. "Is your mama going to keep you safe? She's nowhere in this world."

I'm shrieking, glancing away from his eyes to the empty street all around me. The houses are vacant, lights turned off. Gates dangle open and there isn't a single dog in sight. The tuck shop is barren, its shelves bare.

His hand slips towards the skin revealed by my bunched up shirt. His eyes shift to my waist, little shots of fire spurting from his eyes to my flesh, burning a round mark of desire on my hip.

I open my mouth to scream, "Help me, somebody," but I can't make a sound.

The drunk man's mouth opens wide, laughing, revealing wide teeth, long teeth, changing into a long crocodile snout right in front of my eyes.

"Help!" I screech, hopeless that anybody can hear me from wherever they've gone.

But then—a miracle! Both of us find our eyes riveted to the horizon as a dark-suited figure bobs up and down, moving closer until I recognize the face on the body.

Babamkhulu. My very own grandfather. Fire in his own eyes as he looks at the drunk man holding me captive. Slowly advancing, menacing. At last the drunk man's claws relax and he lets me go.

I come to consciousness, gripping a pillow, the sheets soaked in sweat.

Zi is lying in the other bed, sleeping peacefully, but Gogo is sitting beside me, dipping a washcloth in water and cooling my forehead.

"Khosi, you were somewhere deep," she says now. "I tried to wake you but could not."

I sit up, draping my feet over the edge of the bed. Put my arms around my body and huddle there, hugging knees to chest. I lift my shirt—I'm still wearing the same shirt I was wearing when I drank the herbal remedy—and glance at the skin on my hip where the drunk man's gaze burned me. Though the coin-sized sore he burned in my flesh is gone, there is a small circular shape, black as night, darker than my coffee-colored skin. I've never noticed it before. Was it already here?

I feel like he's branded me, like cattle. Marked me as his.

The nausea is swift and sure and I barely make it to the toilet, bits of bile, chicken, and tomato pouring out of my mouth in a bitter acidic mixture.

Gogo knocks on the door. "Khosi? *Uyagula?* Are you sick?"

"I'm okay," I call, and wait until I hear her shuffling down the hall to the kitchen. In the dark stillness of the house, I hear her turn the burners on to heat water for a cup of tea. She stumbles a little, and finally sits, heavily, in a chair. Its metal legs scrape across the uneven floor.

I sit there in the dark, on the floor of the bathroom, staring up at the box of Omo washing powder we store in the window. What just *happened?*

CHAPTER THIRTEEN

Homecoming

The drunk man starts waiting for me at the taxi stop when Zi and I come home from school. He doesn't say anything to me—he just smiles with his big rotten teeth and follows us home.

One day, Thandi throws little rocks at him. "Leave her alone," she yells. He ducks to avoid the shower of small stones. But still, he follows.

"Big coward," Thandi mutters. "What are you going to do?"

"You don't think I should make him my sugar daddy?" I ask her.

"Are you *crazy*, Khosi?" Thandi shouts. Then she sees I'm teasing. "You've gone mad, girl! I don't think you should make jokes about that man. He's dodgy. You shouldn't ever walk anywhere alone."

"Who's going to walk with me everywhere I need to go?" I ask. "Gogo's too old and Mama's not here most of the time. I just have to learn to protect myself."

But how? I sound brave even while my insides are one big bowl of mushy *phuthu*. The problem is that I don't see a solution. So I have to *act* brave. Of course, I pray to God, hoping that he can hear my prayer out of the millions flooding his ears. Sometimes, I pray to Jesus. At least Jesus was a man and they did terrible things to him before he died. Maybe he understands my fear. Maybe he'll help me, like Babamkhulu.

Thandi glances over her shoulder. The drunk man keeps his distance, but he ambles along, some few houses behind us, running a stick along the metal gates. *Ching ching ching ching.* A chicken darts across the road.

"You need to come get some protective *muthi* from my *gogo*," Thandi advises. "She has *muthi* that can make you invisible to your enemies."

"I'll come get it," I say. "Tomorrow after school."

But that night, Gogo tells me that Mama is finally coming home, after so many weeks—two months—away.

"She will be here tomorrow night," Gogo says. "She said they have given her a three-week holiday."

I'm surprised. It isn't the right month for winter holidays so how did Mama get three weeks off?

"Who is teaching her class while she is gone?" I ask.

"She didn't say. But we must plan a special meal, Khosi." Gogo sounds so excited, like a little girl.

"All Mama's favorites," I agree. "I'll go shopping tomorrow on my way home from school."

The next day, I hurry to pick Zi up as soon as my last class is over. We run through the city streets to catch a taxi back to Imbali.

Zi always says hi to all the women traders sitting on the sidewalk in front of Freedom Square, the ones selling bracelets and necklaces and toys to the people rushing past. Today, we're the ones rushing.

"Don't make me drag you home," I threaten Zi when she falls behind.

"Why are we running, Khosi?" she complains. "I'm tired."

"Mama's coming home today," I remind her. "Don't you want to hurry? Wouldn't it be terrible if Mama arrived home and we weren't there yet?"

Zi's entire face brightens and she shouts at the women, "Mama's coming home! Mama's coming home!"

They wave at her, their special little friend, calling after us, "*Hambani amantombazana! Sheshani!* Hurry hurry hurry!" They shake with laughter when she runs past on her fat little legs.

As our taxi zips out of the city and down the road toward Imbali, the driver turns the music up. I put my fingers in my ears and nudge Zi to do the same. It's too loud to talk so I lose myself in warm thoughts about Little Man. His dreadlocks, so long they reach his shoulders. His *gorgeous* smile.

Actually, I'm a little embarrassed about how often I've been thinking about him lately. At lunch, I'm so shy, even Thandi has asked me if something is wrong. Little Man doesn't say much to me...but it *feels* like he's aware of every move I make. So many times when I look up from my food, our eyes meet.

For the millionth time, I wonder: does he like me?

Zi interrupts my thoughts, poking me in the side. "Look, Khosi, a new advertisement!" she shouts, pointing at a billboard with a cartoon drawing of a man and woman together, embracing on a blue sofa. Large block letters announce: "A man can get AIDS by having sex with an infected woman."

"Shhh." I glance at the other passengers to see if anybody heard. Zi's too young to know you don't talk about these things, not in public.

The taxi turns left, passing the faded red "Coca-Cola! Welcome to Imbali!" billboard that announces the entrance to the township. I tap the side to let the driver know we want to get off and he pulls to a stop right in front of the tuck shop. The drunk man is there again, slumped over on his bucket, wearing the same clothes he always wears. Does he ever go home and change? Does he even have a home to go to? Today, we are able to stop for some few small items for Mama's feast, and then slip by him without his noticing.

On our way to and from the market for vegetables, Zi scares dogs in yards, her usual after-school routine. But today, even over the hectic barking, we hear shouting as we near the house. We both start running, book bags slapping our backs.

As soon as we arrive, we see what the shouting is all about. MaDudu has finally broken the silence of the last weeks. She is standing in the middle of her yard, shaking her broom at Gogo, her flower print apron flapping with each arm movement.

"Your daughter will pay me back," she yells. "Or she'll see what we do to cheats in Imbali."

What is she saying about Mama?

Gogo is huddling in front of the house, waiting for us outside like she always does when the weather is warm. But hearing these words from our neighbor, she retreats into the open door. Even from this distance, I can see her whole body trembling.

The neighbor sweeps vigorously, as though she's sweeping Gogo right out of her yard. She turns around and sees me.

"Hah!" she cries, her voice ugly with triumph. "Khosi, you tell your mother she has nowhere to hide."

"What do you mean, Nkosikazi?" I ask.

"I see what she's up to, I have eyes in the back of my head, spies everywhere." She shakes her finger at me.

"Elizabeth has done nothing but try to help you when your husband died," Gogo says from inside the safety of the house. She's just like me, brave from a distance! I'd be hiding in the house, too. "If you're so angry, talk to her. I'm sure she can explain everything."

"Na, and can she tell my children why they have nothing to show from their father's death?" She grimaces and spits on the ground. "Can she tell me where all the insurance money went? Can she tell me why it disappeared after she helped me?"

"The mouth is a tail to swat away the flies," Gogo says, ushering us through the door. "And it is your mouth that will get us in trouble, Sisi."

But even as we go inside and shut the door, we can still hear the neighbor lady calling after us, her voice like nails shooting through the walls: "I'm not just talking uselessly, Busisiwe Mahlasela! Tell your daughter she can't hide the truth from God."

Gogo sinks into a chair by the door, the scarf that covers her hair shoved to the side. She readjusts it and presses a wobbly hand to her mouth.

We peek outside. MaDudu sees our heads poking through the doorway. She stops sweeping and stares at us until we close the door, leaving just a crack open to let air flow inside.

"Gogo, what's making her so angry?" I ask. It's true that evil is blind but anger is a path in the forest, guiding evil through the dark, right to your doorstep.

Gogo's headscarf flutters in the breeze. "Zi, go watch TV while I talk to your sister," she says. After Zi leaves, the words bleed from her mouth. "Her children think your mother took some of her husband's insurance money after he died!"

"What?" I'm shocked. "What will happen if the neighbor keeps talking like this and everybody believes her?" The thought makes me feel lonely deep inside, at the pit of my stomach. We could be shunned by everybody, if they believe this thing.

"How can she think your mother would cheat somebody who's been a friend and neighbor for so many years?" Gogo crosses her arms under her breasts, looking vulnerable.

"What about the paperwork?" I ask. "It should prove that Mama didn't cheat her."

Gogo clucks her tongue, shakes her head. "She can't read. What good is showing her the paperwork?"

"Maybe she'll forget about it," I say, but we both know you don't forget something like this.

Gogo slumps down in the seat and grabs one of my school folders. She begins to fan herself with it. "It's so hot today, the fish are jumping out of the water."

"Gogo, why don't you wait for Mama outside?" I ask. "It's not so hot out there."

"I don't know..." Gogo trails off, looking anxious.

I peek through the back door at the neighbor's house. "MaDudu has gone inside. She won't be giving you the evil eye anymore."

So Gogo grunts and, slowly, starts to stand up. She struggles so much, I put out my hand to help her, but she waves it away. She likes to be independent.

I understand that, I do. I like to be independent, too.

CHAPTER FOURTEEN

Trouble Between Us

Auntie Phumzi and Mama drive into the yard. I leave the mealie-meal boiling on the stove and run outside just in time to glimpse Zi's skirt flapping up and showing her pink underwear as she runs to greet Mama. It looks like I need to buy her longer skirts, to protect her from dirty old men.

Then Mama gets out of the car. She has lost so much weight, her face is wrinkled, the skin sagging off her jowls—like she suddenly became really old, overnight. Her ankle wobbles as it hits the ground, as if her legs are still adjusting to the lost flesh.

Zi stops. She backs away.

Gogo is so surprised, she exclaims, "Pho! Who are you? Who took my daughter? Where is Elizabeth?"

"I told her she's trying to be like the white women who think it is beautiful to be a skeleton," Auntie Phumzi says, laughing to make light of our fear.

"It is just that I have been so sick, Mama," Mama explains. "I was even sick when I came home last visit, but I did not want to worry you."

"There is sick but this?" Gogo sweeps her hand towards Mama.

"I didn't think I could handle the long trip back from Greytown," she says. She holds her arms out for Zi. "Aren't you going to say hi to me, Zinhle?"

That's when Zi finally goes to her. But as Mama wraps her arms around Zi's little body, Zi starts weeping and howling. Mama looks over at us, her eyes and body saying "Help" even though she doesn't say the word. Then she sees me. "Nomkhosi," she says, her voice gentle. "How are you?"

"Mama, come inside and take a seat." I am confused and ashamed to see Mama like this, so thin like the men and women who die of AIDS.

Mama wobbles, her movement constricted by Zi's arms wrapped tight around her.

"Elizabeth!" We all turn at the sound of someone calling Mama's name. MaDudu is hobbling towards the fence that separates our houses, moaning like a woman in pain.

"What's wrong?" Mama asks before we can stop her.

As soon as she has our attention, MaDudu starts shouting. "You thought you could cheat an old woman, Elizabeth," she cries.

"What—what are you talking about?" Mama asks.

MaDudu grips the fence, her face close to the metal wires. "The leg has no nose, Elizabeth!" she cackles. "You see, your sins *always* find you out. Already, you are suffering because of what you have done!"

"Hush now, Themba Dudu." Gogo's voice is harsh and angry.

Zi whimpers.

"But what are you talking about?" Mama's face loses color. Her cheeks, the color of ashes. "What have I done?"

Gogo steps in front of Mama, as if she wants to hide her from the accusations, but MaDudu paws at her arms, trying to face Mama directly.

"You have done enough damage with your anger," Gogo says. "There is no trouble between us but you will make trouble with all your accusations."

"There *is* trouble between us," MaDudu's words are high and pinched and strangled. "*Yebo, impela*, trouble indeed. Don't deny it!"

She claws past Gogo and suddenly the two old women are shoving each other as Mama retreats, her feet slipping on the gravel. Auntie Phumzi helps her up and the two of them hurry into the house.

Gogo is old but she has tremendous strength and will in those arms of hers. She doesn't let go of MaDudu even as I force my body in between them.

"Gogo, go inside," I yell.

MaDudu grabs a chunk of my hair and yanks. "It's because of your mother that I'm hungry." She spits, right in my face, shouting at the closed door, "Where is my money, Elizabeth? You can't hide it forever! God will find you out!"

We're so close, face to face, MaDudu fuming in my arms. We look each other in the eye and the anger in hers spills over like mealie-meal boiling over the side of a pot.

I close my eyes and will my whole body to become a secret, shutting off the tunnel that leaks emotion from my heart to my eyes.

"Please go home, Nkosikazi," I say, opening my eyes.

"Go home to *what?*" She sighs, as if she's giving up. "To an empty cupboard?"

"If you're hungry, we have food we can give you."

And finally she sags in my arms, a feeble weight. My arms close around her body, so natural, almost a hug. *She's so afraid*, I realize as I touch her. *She's so afraid and so hurt.*

But then she stiffens, like I spoke my thoughts out loud. "I'll return, Khosi," she threatens, "and I'll be better prepared next time. You tell your mother."

I watch her shamble back to her own yard before I go inside.

Gogo is fretting over Mama, who sinks into the sofa like an old weak woman—as if *she's* the grandmother. "Don't pay any attention to her, Elizabeth," Gogo says. "She's just a crazy old woman."

"The very idea, that I would steal money from her," Mama says.

"Welcome home, Elizabeth," Auntie Phumzi jokes. "I'm sure *now* you're sorry you stayed away so long. Look at all the excitement you were missing!"

Zi starts giggling and can't stop until Mama says, "That's enough, Zi," her voice sharp, not the same old gentle Mama we've always known. She reaches up to pat her head. "Sho! Where's my headscarf? It's missing!"

"I'm sure it's just out in the yard," I say, quick quick, trying to prevent alarm even as Gogo sucks in her breath with sudden fear. "I'll look for it."

But the front yard is empty. So is the street. I even search MaDudu's yard by peering in through her gate. Nothing. No scarf.

"It doesn't matter," Mama says, looking exhausted. She closes her eyes.

I look over at Gogo for comfort but all I see is my fear mirrored back.

I sit on a chair near the sofa and rock back and forth, pressing my hands against my lips so I don't blurt out, "It does matter, Mama! You could be in danger!"

MaDudu is so angry, she might be willing to do something evil. If she took Mama's headscarf...if she took some of my hair when she pulled it...she could use either of those things to harm us.

Mama closes her eyes. "Yo! I'm so tired. I've been working *too* hard."

In just a few seconds, she's already asleep. I cover her with a blanket and tiptoe into the kitchen, where Auntie Phumzi has taken over the cooking from Gogo. "Do you think MaDudu took her scarf?" I whisper.

"Let's hope it just blew away in the wind," Gogo mutters.

But the night is still, like a photograph, nothing moving, not even a single insect disturbing the air.

I watch my family going through the evening rituals, Auntie Phumzi clattering dishes in the kitchen, Gogo and Zi watching TV while they wait for food. Usually Auntie is in her own home, cooking for her own husband and children, and it's me in the kitchen. And usually, when Mama comes home from her job on the weekends, she's lively, full of dance and song, waltzing Zi around the house and chiding me for something I forgot to do while she was away. But here she is, already asleep.

Some homecoming!

It makes me feel...homesick. Homesick and here I am, at home, surrounded by the people I love.

I step outside to escape the feeling.

MaDudu has gone inside. But if she were standing in front of me, would I say the words that are flooding my mind? *I'll be watching you. And if you dare do anything evil to my family, if you dare try to curse us, I'll come after you. I don't know how but I have friends and they'll help me.*

Looking at the quiet neighborhood, the warning seems really crazy.

CHAPTER FIFTEEN

Muthi for Mama

A nightmare interrupts my sleep again that night. In it, Mama has made a bargain with the devil.

"It's just a small thing, Khosi," she pleads with me. "It is just so that you and Gogo and Zi will be safe when I am gone."

"A bargain with the devil is never a small thing, Mama, you know that." I look at her, helpless, but she looks away.

"It is necessary," she says.

And when we are asleep, the devil comes. He is big as a whale, opening his mouth wide and swallowing us whole, house and all. Gogo, Zi, and I wake up, deep inside his belly, wondering how long we have before we will die. It's hot and humid down there and the air is thin, eaten up by fire. Already, Gogo's face is ash-gray as she struggles to breathe, and Zi is beginning to fade as her body is wrung of all its water.

I wake up sweating, sitting bolt upright in bed. *What are you trying to tell me?* I ask Babamkhulu, looking at his picture hanging over Gogo's bed.

I look at my mother, sleeping beside me. She has lost so much weight, her face is wrinkled, not smooth like it always was.

"Mama, what is going on?" I whisper. "Why are the ancestors bothering me with all these dreams about you?"

Of course, she does not hear me. She is sleeping too soundly.

In the morning, Gogo sends me off to the *sangoma's* to find out what's wrong with Mama, and to see if she has some herbs that will give Mama an appetite.

"Mama won't like it," I say.

"I cannot just sit by while my daughter starves to death," Gogo says.

We both look at Mama, already asleep on the sofa even though she only woke some few minutes ago. She just stumbled out of bed and then lay down on the sofa, shaking her head when I asked her if she wanted breakfast.

We walk outside and Gogo calls the woman across the street to ask her if she will accompany me up the hill. "My granddaughter has become a magnet for troublesome men," she says. "I'd prefer if she doesn't go alone."

"One minute, Mama," the woman says, and goes inside. She comes back with a scarf and her four-year-old.

"So the *tsotsis* like you, eh, *Ntombi?*" the woman asks, shaking her head. "Ah, there are so many of these men hanging around Imbali, with nothing better to do than to bother young girls like you. No wonder your grandmother is afraid."

"Oh, those *tsotsis* just yell at me, Sisi," I say. "It's this one older man I'm having a hard time avoiding."

"*Ncese,* shame." The woman drags the word out. "I don't know what these men are thinking. You're just a child."

The two of us trudge up the hill, talking about everyday things and what what what, nothing important. She is a good neighbor; she doesn't even ask why I'm going to visit a *sangoma.* You don't talk about these things because it could be something shameful.

That is true in our case. It is embarrassing that Mama has lost so much weight. People will be talking next, saying she has the disease of these days. So if our neighbor asked, I would say, "Zi has a cold," or "Gogo's bones ache," or something like that. I would never say why I am really going.

When we reach the *sangoma's,* the neighbor points to a nearby house, "My sister lives just there. When you are done, come find me and we will walk home together."

I pass through Thandi's metal gate, noticing the new white sign, with the misspelled word announcing: "Brothers and Sisters, we are abel to cure any sick." I know I should run inside and say hello to Thandi, but I am not up for any questions, especially if she asks how Mama is doing. I cannot tell her the truth, and I do not want to lie.

Thankfully, there is no queue and I crawl into the hut to see Makhosi quick quick.

I tell her about Mama. "She's tired, Gogo," I say. "Tired and stressed."

Makhosi regards me for some few seconds. "Is she eating?"

I start to cry. "Oh, Gogo, she's lost so much weight." My voice drops to a whisper. "She looks like the men and women who die."

"Has she gone to see a doctor?"

I shake my head. How funny, my mother who believes in science and doctors has failed to see one for her sickness.

"*Hayibo!* She must go to a doctor." Makhosi moves fast. She mixes herbs together and wraps them in a newspaper packet. "Twice a day, steep a big spoonful of these herbs in a cup of boiling water. Your mama must drink it every morning and every night. These herbs will calm her down and give her an appetite, which will give her energy."

"Thank you," I say.

"Tell her it's very important that she eats, even if she doesn't feel like it, to gain back her strength. Tell her it's very important she goes to see a doctor."

"I'll tell her," I promise, wondering how mad Mama will be when I present her with herbs from a *sangoma*—herbs and advice to go see a medical doctor.

I hand Makhosi fifty *rand* for the medicine, wondering if I should tell her about the latest developments in my life. But I am ashamed to reveal our neighbor's accusations. It is one thing to tell her that a witch has been stalking me. It is another to tell her that somebody thinks Mama stole money.

"Are you worried about something else?" Makhosi asks.

"No, everything's fine," I say, feeling just as terrible denying it as I would admitting it.

"And the dreams? Are the ancestors still bothering you when you sleep, Khosi?"

I look down at the mud floor. "Sometimes, Gogo. But it is getting better."

She's still sitting there when I squat down and crawl through the entrance to leave.

I don't know why I lied to her, when her spirits will surely reveal the truth. But I don't want to admit how many of the dreams involve Mama. Then she might think Mama is sick because God is punishing her for her sins. Then she'll wonder what Mama has done that is so bad, when I'm sure she's done nothing wrong.

CHAPTER SIXTEEN

Eyes Do Not See All

Mama sits in the kitchen singing while I chop vegetables for Saturday's supper. All afternoon I've been cooking, trying to tempt her appetite, but she pushes each dish away with one word: "*Ngisuthi*." How can she be full when she eats nothing?

Zi leans against her, hand in her mouth, while Mama picks out the knots in her hair and sings. "*Siyahamb' ekukhanyen' kwenkhos'*. We are walking in the light of God."

During Mama's absence, Zi's hair tangled up in thick knots. I fill a basin with warm water so that Mama can wash Zi's hair while I cook. Zi lies on the floor as Mama pours water over her hair into the basin. She washes it three times while I chop vegetables.

"Zi, are you trying to grow dreads like those tough guys that hang out in front of Mama Thambo's *shebeen*? Are you trying to be a *tsotsi*?" Mama jokes, her eyes shining at us. Zi giggles. "You're such a sweet, pretty girl. You don't need to be a gangster."

"It isn't just *tsotsis* that wear dreadlocks," I say, thinking of Little Man. "There are some nice young men with dreads."

"Does this nice young man with dreads have a name, hey, Khosi?" Mama asks.

"Mama! No! Don't be silly!" The last thing I want is for them to find out about Little Man. That's just the thing to get me in trouble when I haven't even done anything wrong.

"Sho! Look at this." Mama holds up a big chunk of Zi's hair, dripping with soap and water.

"What happened?" I ask.

"Her hair is so brittle, it just broke off in my hand," Mama says.

Zi struggles to sit up. "I'm going to look like Uncle Richard," she says, seeing her hair dripping in Mama's hand. We all laugh even more. Uncle Richard is completely bald.

"You need to take better care of her hair while I'm gone, Khosi," Mama chides me, cutting one of the knots off with scissors. "And she needs to wear a scarf at night."

"I know, Mama," I say, like I always do. But we both know Zi won't let us touch her hair when Mama's gone. She won't wear a scarf to bed. She won't even listen to Gogo when Gogo tries to get her to behave.

I slice up a big pumpkin into a large pan, fill it with water, and put it on the stove to boil. I chop tomatoes and pepper, take rice off the stove, and dish everything up with chicken and gravy, placing one plate in front of Gogo and another in front of Mama. "See, Mama? All your favorites so when you go back to work, you'll go with a nice full stomach and good memories of home."

"Shame, all this nice food," she says. "I wish I could stay here always, where my daughter takes such good care of me, instead of going back to Greytown where I must work so hard. I wish I had a better appetite."

That sounds like an invitation, so after I set a plate in front of Zi, I boil some water and steep the herbs in it, as the *sangoma* directed. I strain the herbs out, pour the tea into a mug, and set it near Mama's plate.

"What what what?" she asks. "What is this, Khosi?"

"It's supposed to help you eat, Mama." I glance from her to Gogo. I've always been taught to be obedient to both of them, but what do I do when they disagree? Who do I obey first—Mama or Gogo? "It's just herbs. It's nothing to worry about. Completely natural!"

"Did you send her to the *sangoma*?" Mama asks and sighs when Gogo nods.

"Drink it," I say. "Please, Mama."

"Please, Elizabeth," Gogo urges.

Mama watches my face carefully. "Well, I don't suppose it'll do any harm. Perhaps it might do some good. Herbal remedies have some value."

She gulps it down, just as if it tastes bad. But I've already tasted it and it tastes delicious, just like peppermint and lemons.

Mama hands the mug back. "I'll drink this," she tells Gogo. "But I don't want you sending Khosi to the *sangoma* again. I don't want her head filled with nonsense."

Gogo starts whispering to me, so that Mama won't hear. "Your mama is a very wonderful woman but she doesn't know everything," she says. "Eyes do not see all. The *sangoma* can see things that we cannot see."

"Stop whispering," Mama snaps. "I know exactly what you're trying to do but I want Khosi and Zi to be modern Zulu women. I don't want them dependent on superstition—or on men."

Gogo's mouth is one long thin line, like she's sewn it shut from the inside. But she doesn't say anything else.

CHAPTER SEVENTEEN

PUNISHMENT

I'm glad Mama doesn't go to church that Sunday. Because she's lost so much weight, I just know those old ladies would gossip about her, judging, as if they know anything about Mama! That is what I see every Sunday. I don't know if it is jealousy or a mean spirit or what what what, but it troubles me.

That Sunday, the poor woman they pick on is Zolani Ngcuka.

Zolani is only a few years older than me but she already has a husband and a baby. She's a beautiful woman and wears the church uniform; she sways in the aisles and claps when we sing, dancing like she wishes she was in a Zionist congregation.

But this Sunday, when she enters, the people shake their heads. Actually, there is a collective gasp as she limps into her pew.

She hasn't been to mass for weeks and weeks and weeks. And during that time, she's lost too much weight; her clothes fall off her like she's just a stick. Her cheeks look like she's sucked in her breath. There are little bloody bumps all over her scalp.

During the passing of the peace, people refuse to shake her hand or kiss her. They don't greet her, calling out, "*Sawubona*, Sisi!" No, they look away.

After mass, I hear those same ladies clucking like old chickens in the courtyard. Losing weight, it means one thing only in our minds—the disease of these days. And that's what they talk about, even if they don't call it by its name. I understand why they don't say it out loud. Just saying the word—HIV—is like uttering a curse.

"I can tell you are a good girl," one of them says to Thandi as we pass, grabbing her arm and squeezing. "Good girls are always fat."

It's true, Thandi is shaped like a ball of butter. Her smile disappears deep in her fat cheeks, round like a baby's. But the problem with being fat is that men love it. And then it's hard to be a good girl.

"But why doesn't Zolani take the medicine?" I whisper to Thandi. Like those old ladies, we're standing in the courtyard gossiping. "They say if you take the medicine, you can get better. You gain the weight back. The sores go away. They say the disease isn't a death sentence anymore! Maybe you don't live forever, but you don't die right away either."

I'm thinking of Mama. All the weight she's lost. Could *she* be HIV positive? It's not possible. Unless...unless Thandi's right, and Baba does have other girlfriends on the side. It could happen. It's very common for Zulu men to have more than one girlfriend. Just like in the old days, they married more than one wife if they could afford it.

I feel a sudden spurt of anger at Baba. Then I try to calm it. After all, I know nothing. There are other reasons Mama could have lost weight, hey? But I can't think of any.

Thandi shrugs. "That medicine doesn't work for everybody."

"*Why not?*" The injustice stings me to the core. Zolani is so young and her baby is so young. Why would God let her die when other people live?

"Maybe a witch cursed her and she hasn't gone to see a *sangoma* to remove the curse," Thandi explains. "Maybe it was too late by the time she started taking the medicine."

"That's what happened to my uncle Jabulani," I say. "He waited and waited and then he got full-blown AIDS. The medicine didn't help him then."

Though the other ladies ignore Zolani after the service, Gogo doesn't. As we pass out of the yard to walk home, she grasps Zolani's hand, looks her in the eyes, and says, "God bless you, child. We're praying for you every day." She says it in a loud voice, like she's scolding the other old ladies.

I take Zolani's thin hand in mine. Something in her skin feels pale and cold and hungry, like a child weeping out in the streets, begging people for something to eat. The sound of that same voice is *crying* in the lines of Zolani's palm as they meet mine.

I'm so surprised, I drop her hand.

Then I quickly grab it again, so she doesn't think I'm like those ladies who judge her. I bring my other hand up to grasp hers in both hands.

Rub her hands together to warm them, whispers a voice in my ear.

I look around to see who spoke to me, but nobody's there—only Gogo with a question in her eyes.

I rub Zolani's hands together, gently, gradually becoming more vigorous. And for some few seconds, it really feels like I'm helping her. The sobbing I hear in her hands ceases.

Maybe that's all she really needed—to be touched. Sometimes, isn't touch healing?

Pray a blessing for her, that the power of God and the protection of the ancestors is with her, whispers that voice. It sounds like a command.

"I'll be praying for you, Sisi," I mumble.

Looking at her baby—tied to her back with a bright red, green, and yellow cloth—makes me feel sad for a reason I can't think about.

Death is not something that is natural, something that we should just accept, just like that, especially when someone is so young. You must do something about it. And if you know somebody is going to die, you must do something about it before they're gone.

"Thank you, Sisi," she says. She grips my hand like...like she's holding on to something she needs. "Stay well, Sisi."

I open my mouth to respond, "Go well, Sisi," but nothing comes out. A thin, silvery shadow hovers just above her body when she turns her head.

I release her hand. What is that shadow? Is it her spirit, already leaving the body? It floats just above her as she walks away from us down the road to her house.

I look at Gogo, wondering if she can see Zolani's spirit leaving her body, but Gogo is examining her own hands. "Do you remember her wedding, Khosi?" she asks.

I remember. It was a beautiful wedding, the kind all girls dream about. She had a huge Catholic service, with a big mass and a reception afterward. She was dressed all in white, and their cake was just like the cakes you see in American movies—three tiers, with lots of white frosting. Her family is so Catholic, the groom didn't even *lobola* her! The women of Imbali had plenty to say about that, believe me. "They've forgotten that they're Zulu," they said, and, "Is it even marriage if the groom doesn't pay her parents *something?*" But there were others who pointed out that at least she got married. "Sho! so many young people don't even bother getting married at all. Then who do the children belong to?"

"Since she's married, why do the women say she's not a good girl?" I ask Gogo even though I already know the answer. I just wish somebody would say it out loud. It seems like we have so many secrets in Imbali.

"She is so young, so young." That's all Gogo will say. She purses her lips together as she regards the gossiping ladies in the courtyard. "Ehe! We must pray for her, Khosi. At church, we will pray to God and to the saints in communion with us. But at home, we must pray to the ancestors, because they're also in communion with us. Maybe they'll help her. Maybe they'll help all of us."

"I hope so," I say. "Gogo, why do you think so many people in South Africa are sick with this thing?"

"I don't know," Gogo says. "But sometimes I wonder why we blacks are being punished when we have already suffered for so long."

CHAPTER EIGHTEEN

Your Sins Will Find You Out

MaDudu is waiting for us when we return from church, clutching her metal gate.

The dim whispering I heard when I saw Zolani's spirit lift up and away from her body is back, voices scurrying around in my head the way chickens are darting around her feet. *Help us*, I plead, unsure who I'm pleading to. Everybody, I guess. God, Jesus, the ancestors.

Are the ancestors really speaking to me? Is it their voices I hear, whispering? They do not speak to just anyone. But I can't hear what they're saying over the noise she is making as we hurry past and inside our gate.

"You think going to church makes you good?" she taunts us. "You think going to church makes up for your thievery?"

I pat Zi's backside, ushering her inside, while Gogo turns around and faces our accuser, her voice pleading. "Sisi, what is this thing of anger between us?"

We stand in the doorway, halfway in, halfway out. The doorway is where the ancestors linger. It is a place of healing. Those whispers grow stronger, swirling around my head like a strong wind.

But just how the ancestors can mend MaDudu's anger, I don't know. *Please do something*, I beg.

"Ask your daughter Elizabeth what this thing of anger is," MaDudu says, spitting on the ground.

"The tongue of an angry woman brings nothing but evil," Gogo says.

But MaDudu starts screaming. "Give an old woman justice," she screeches, at the top of her lungs. "Give an old woman her money!"

Dread clamps its strong hand around my stomach. I glance around and realize that neighbors have started to gather in little groups, watching the spectacle of two *gogos* shouting at each other. Two women pause in the middle of the road, openly staring. A little girl walks over to the fence and grabs it, poking her face up to the metal so she can see better.

"Gogo, let's go inside," I murmur, realizing that whatever else is going to happen today, nothing good can come of shouting at each other publicly.

Mama hobbles to the door, looking old and grey and tired. She pushes us aside and limps outside. "What is all this yelling?" she asks.

MaDudu grins at her, barring old yellowed teeth. "Eh-he, I told you, you would suffer because of your sins. See how thin you have grown? See how sickness takes over your body? God is punishing you for what you have done."

"Go back inside, Elizabeth," Gogo murmurs. "We should ignore her."

But Mama grows angry, and an angry Mama doesn't ignore things. We all know this. Mama gathers up all her strength and marches over to the fence separating our yard from the Dudus' yard.

"If I took your money, where is it, hah?" she shouts. "Look at our old house. Look at that sagging roof. See how the paint peels? If I had money, do you not think I would do something about this place we live in?"

"Oh, you are just talk talk talk," MaDudu says. Her eyes glitter fury as she stares at us. "But the house of the loud talker leaks. You can't fool me. You are like a bird, hiding things in your nest. That money is somewhere and I will find it."

"You are an old, foolish woman," Gogo says. "You will bring evil on all of us with your anger."

"No, I am not the one bringing evil on us," MaDudu says.

"*Wozani*," Gogo says, opening her arms wide as if gathering me and Mama inside and sweeping us into the house.

I lean against the door as Gogo sinks onto the sofa, trembling. Mama stands in the middle of the dining room, as if she is so tired, she doesn't even remember that she should sit.

The next day, the drunk man is lounging against the fence when Zi and I get off the taxi, his arms crossed, his entire posture casual. He grins and starts walking towards us. "Let's run," I tell Zi.

He doesn't bother chasing after us but his laughter follows us down the road.

On Tuesday, we stay on the taxi instead of getting off at our usual stop. We stop near Thandi's house instead and circle back around in a different direction.

We avoid him that day but on Wednesday, he's lurking at our gate when we arrive.

"Can't you just leave me alone?" I scream.

The noise brings MaDudu to her front yard. She laughs to see me trying to figure out how to get into my gate without that drunk man grabbing me.

"I told your mother," she calls. "I told her, your sins follow you."

"What sin have I committed?" I ask her, fuming now, glancing from him to her and back to Zi, calculating. How quick do I need to be to get us both safely inside the yard?

"Not you," she says. "Your mother."

"Am I paying for my mother's sins?" I snap.

"We all pay for our mother's sins," she responds.

Maybe she's right. Maybe we have sinned. It seems obvious we've done something so that the ancestors have lifted their protection. Or, if we're innocent, something has been done to us to block their protection.

The thought makes me so furious that I become bold. Shoving Zi behind me, I march right up to that man and shove him aside, slapping his hands away from my hips as he reaches out to grab me. As I unlock the gate, he grasps me and twirls me around until I'm facing him, staring at his rotten tooth in the center of his mouth, noticing how his rotten tooth and the witch's gold tooth are the exact same tooth.

"Get inside the gate, Zi," I shout, wrenching myself out of his hands and dashing in, slamming it shut in his face.

"I will come for you just now, *Ntombi*," he calls as he walks away. "I will come for you."

The words sound familiar, dim echoes from something said to me long ago, but I can't place it.

I glare at MaDudu and finally say what I should have said weeks ago. "If it's true that we're punished for our sins, you and that man had better watch out. You are opening the door for evil to slip right inside."

"Are you threatening me?" She spits on the ground. "Any sins I commit are nothing compared to your mother's."

I grab the fence with my hand and shake it. But that's all I dare do.

Once inside, I remember suddenly why the drunk man's words sound so familiar. Why, it's the same thing the witch said to me some few months ago, the day our neighbor buried her husband.

CHAPTER NINETEEN

Lying to Mama

Uncle Richard comes home the following weekend, the week of Little Man's party. I wait until Uncle has a nice, full stomach before asking if I can go to Thandi's for the evening.

"We have a school project," I lie, my stomach feeling empty even though I'm filling it with a big plate of *phuthu* and chicken.

"*Hawu!* A school project on a Friday night?" Uncle Richard asks.

"Thandi won't be home tomorrow so we need to work on it tonight."

"Khosi, it isn't safe for you to be out alone after dark," Mama says. "Think of that drunk man who accosted you when I was home two months ago."

"Thandi's father will walk me home."

Uncle Richard puts his plate on his lap and stares at me, as if he knows I am lying. He's a big man, with a big belly. Even though he's bald, his face has always reminded me of Mama's. "You're not like your mother when she was your age, eh?" He jabs the air with his fingers. "You're not sneaking out to meet some young man, eh?"

"Richard!" Mama says. "Don't make her think about doing these things."

I'm relieved for the distraction. "Baba told me you were wild, Mama! Did you sneak out to meet young men?"

Mama looks ashamed, and then she laughs, a laugh that turns into a cough. We wait patiently until she stops coughing and regains her breath.

"Only once," she says at last. "My brothers caught me and gave me a beating I'll never forget."

"We're too soft on girls these days," Uncle Richard says.

"Perhaps you mean *I'm* too soft on *my* girls," Mama says. She smiles at me, and the smile is warm. "Khosi's a good girl. She has never needed a beating and even if she did, I couldn't do that to my child."

Should lying be so easy? I wonder.

"Anyway," Mama continues, "Khosi's too young for men."

"Because she's the daughter of our household, we think so," Uncle Richard says, "but there are many men who will not think she's too young for these things. They're ready now to take advantage of her innocence."

"It's true," Gogo says. She's eating with her hands and now she shakes a food-covered finger at Mama. "And if I remember anything about your childhood, Elizabeth, it's only going to get worse when Khosi decides *she* likes men."

Mama laughs. "Hey hey! What a thing!" She shakes her head. "Don't you let any young men fall in love with you, hey, Khosi?"

"Don't worry, Mama," I reassure her. "I'm too young to fall in love and get married."

"Who said anything about getting married?" Mama asks.

My face turns warm. It's true, at night I dream about a big church wedding with a white dress and a big white cake. And of course, Little Man down at the altar. I'm always grateful for sweet dreams, the kind that don't wake me, sweating and shaking, afraid to go back to sleep.

Mama hands her plate to me. "*Ngisuthi*," she says.

"But you hardly ate," I protest. There's a mountain of *phuthu* left on her plate.

"*Ngisuthi*," she repeats and begins to cough.

I'm not supposed to question my elders, so I scrape her food into the rubbish bin. But we all stare at her while she coughs and coughs and coughs. She holds her hand to her mouth like she's afraid her lungs are going to fall out if she doesn't keep them in.

"Sisi, it isn't like you to eat nothing," Uncle Richard says. "And this coughing, I don't like it. You must go to the doctor."

"I've been to the clinic in Greytown," Mama explains. "I waited and waited for hours and I never even saw a nurse. I grew so tired waiting, I slept all the next day and missed a second day of work. I can't do it again."

"I'll go with you, Mama," I say. "Then you don't have to wait in line. You can sit and rest while I wait."

"We'll see," she says.

"Did you have to wait long to see the doctor when you were young, Gogo?" I ask.

Gogo laughs—*hee-hee-hee*—like what I said tickles her. "There were no doctors in my village when I was a girl," she says, "so we went to the *sangoma* instead. There was a missionary hospital a few hours away. Sometimes they would send a doctor to our village for a week. The line would stretch all the way through the village and beyond!"

"It was a hard life," Uncle Richard says. "You and Zi are lucky to grow up in the new South Africa."

"I don't think we're so lucky, Uncle Richard." I've washed the last dish so I take Zi on my lap and we sit together on the chair near Gogo. "People still have a hard life these days."

"Khosi, you can't know what it was like to live here when 'black' was a curse word," he says.

"That's true." I don't know what it was like to live under apartheid. I only know the history. And the aftermath—what it's been like to grow up in the new South Africa.

"You don't know all the problems we suffered for so many years," he says.

"No, I just see all the problems of today."

"Khosi," Mama rebukes me. "Don't be disrespectful."

"I'm sorry, Uncle," I apologize.

"No, Khosi's right," he tells Mama. "The past is important but so is today."

I don't say it, but I think today is even more important than yesterday. Yesterday's gone—but what problems have we conquered? In the past, we lacked freedom, there weren't any jobs, and people were dying because of the liberation war. But there still aren't any jobs and now we're dying because of AIDS. As for the future? I wish I knew what it might bring. Its blankness stretching out before us scares me.

Maybe Gogo knows I'm holding back. She leans forward and takes my face in her hands without a word exchanged between us.

"You can go to school, *mntwana wam'*," she says. "You can be a teacher or a nurse or even a doctor. There will always be trouble in this life. But your life will never be so hard as mine. You are indeed lucky."

CHAPTER TWENTY

LITTLE MAN'S PARTY

Uncle walks me to Thandi's house. "If Thandi's *baba* cannot walk you home, call me when you are done, and I will come fetch you," he says at the gate.

"Yes, Uncle," I agree and go inside.

"Oh, aren't you so excited?" Thandi greets me. "Your first party!"

Actually, Thandi is more excited than I am. My emotions are a nest of troubled snakes, slithering and sliding around in my stomach.

When we are certain that Uncle Richard is far away, we leave for Little Man's house. Thandi's *baba* isn't even home to bother us, to ask, "Where are you going?" and "When will you return?" It is nothing like my house.

"Where is your *baba*?" I ask as we walk through the already darkened streets. Even though I am not alone, I feel skittish, hoping we don't meet the drunk man who likes to bother me, or a *tsotsi*, or—well—*anybody* who might give us trouble.

"He's off to see his girlfriend," Thandi says.

"And your mama?"

"She's visiting her sister in Ulundi."

I would not be so casual if I knew my *baba* had a girlfriend. But it's true, what Thandi said to me some few weeks ago, what do I know? Baba lives with his mother, and we only see him some few times a year. He could have another family—other daughters, maybe a son—and how would we know?

I shake those thoughts off. If Mama doesn't worry, why should I?

People are spilling out of Little Man's yard and have overtaken the road. A car is trying to pass. The driver beeps his horn but people are slow to part.

I'm not used to seeing so many men gathered in one place with so few women to entertain them. Some few lucky men have found a girl and are dancing to music in the center of the yard. The rest stand in little groups around the perimeter, holding drinks.

"*Mfaaan*'," Thandi drawls, speaking to the man who attaches himself to her side as soon as we arrive. "Khosi, this is Honest."

Honest is short with big fat cheeks, handsome but flabby. Even though he looks young, there are telltale wrinkles, barely visible, just around his eyes. Yes, this man is definitely too old for Thandi. I wish she would listen when I tell her things like that.

He nuzzles her neck and whispers to her and then they disappear.

Now I'm all alone. As I scan the yard, looking for Little Man, three men surround me. "Do you want to dance?" one of them asks.

I look from one grin to the other. They have big mouths with big white teeth.

Go away, I think. Remembering the lie I told my family so I could come to this party makes me feel suddenly homesick. *I just want to go home.*

A man comes up to me from behind, slips his arm around me, and steers me into the circle of men and women dancing. When I look up into his face, I realize it's the drunk man by the tuck shop.

"Hey," I shout, startled.

He grins, revealing the big rotten tooth in the center of his large, toothy mouth. "Your mama's not here now," he says, "so we can have a good time."

"I don't know how to dance," I protest, slipping out of his arms and moving off to the side.

He catches my arm with his hand and swings me back towards him in a tight embrace. "It doesn't matter. You're so pretty." He squeezes my waist. "I know you want to have a good time."

"No, I really don't." My protest feels feeble.

"If I was handsome, would you still say that?" he asks, blowing hot stinky breath towards me. He lowers his face close to mine and whispers, "I can be young and handsome in the dark."

Somebody get me out of here.

"Let me go." My voice is low but insistent.

His eyes are small and mean and hard and drunk as he grips me tighter, his groin digging and grinding into my hip. "Can I come visit you sometime?" He laughs. "Will *your mama* let me come inside?"

He doesn't even know my name and he's already making lewd comments. Am I that unimportant to him, just a warm body to squeeze? Just a bunch of meat that he wants to gobble up with his big crocodile teeth?

"Let me go," I repeat, my voice louder as his hands grasp my hips, slipping low, then crawling back up again and clutching hard, his fingers tight like claws.

The men nearby laugh at the way I'm struggling against him, like this is all a game. What is *wrong* with them? Why don't they help me?

Echoes of Mama's voice sliver through my head. *Don't you ever let yourself be a victim, Khosi.* If nobody is going to help me, I realize, I have to help myself. "You're disgusting," I shriek. "Leave me alone!"

He's so startled, he lets go. I stumble backwards, smacking right into Little Man. His arms close around me, awkward, light, his voice against my hair. "Are you okay?"

Pulling back just enough to see his face, I smile at him, lips trembling with my voice. "This man keeps bothering me."

"Hey, she's with me," the man protests. "We were dancing."

"Go away, my friend," Little Man says. "She doesn't want to dance with you."

He shoves Little Man and grabs me. "I'm not through with you, *Ntombi*," he growls.

"But *she's* through with you," Little Man says, elbowing his way between us.

Suddenly, my rescuers are everywhere, glaring at my attacker, surrounding us in a close circle. He releases me and staggers off.

"You need to be careful, Khosi," Little Man scolds me, like a big brother. "Some of these men have been drinking *utshwala* and beer all afternoon. They're *drunk*." He weaves around like a drunk man, lurching into the wall, then sliding to the ground. He reaches up his hand and pulls me down to sit beside him.

And there we are, sitting next to each other, our hands still touching lightly. I'm conscious of each finger stroking mine.

"What's your brother celebrating?" I ask, even though I already know.

"His new job, hey? He found one only six months after passing matric."

"Congratulations. So you slaughtered a goat to thank the ancestors?"

"Yah," Little Man says. "We already did the ceremony, going through the house, beating the drums. My mother spent the last week brewing *utshwala*. There is enough *utshwala* in the house for an entire *impi* to drink!"

Utshwala is more than just beer, it is ritual food. And when the men drink it at a party like this, they are drinking to thank the ancestors for something, in this case, the family's good luck that Little Man's brother found a job. But they also drink strong beer and that's what makes them so drunk.

We're silent again, nothing to say. I laugh just to break the silence, and then I feel stupid, laughing for no reason like that.

"You want to dance?" Little Man asks.

"I think I've had enough dancing for tonight."

"We can just sit here and talk then."

Maybe I would've agreed to that, but when I look up to smile at him, my eyes are drawn to the corner of the yard, where my stalker is sitting, glowering at me.

"I should go home," I say. "My family doesn't even know I'm here."

"Oh, don't go yet," he says.

My heart speeds up at the tone in his voice, the pleading look he offers. "Okay, I'll stay a little longer."

"You'll feel more comfortable if you have a drink." He stands, reaching a hand out to help me up. He puts his hand on my waist and steers me through the door.

I like the way his hand fits right there, lightly touching the extra flesh on my waist. But what would Gogo do if she saw it? And what will Little Man's mother say if she sees it? Surely she's around somewhere. This thought makes me step away from him as we walk through the house, a sudden chill on my skin where his hand rested.

He stops before a large tin pot. "Would you like some *utshwala?*" he jokes.

I laugh with him. Young women don't drink *utshwala*. It is for men and *gogos* only.

He opens the refrigerator. "Lemonade or cold drink?"

"Lemonade."

I watch as he pours for me. No man has ever poured me a drink before. It's always me, serving Baba or my uncles and cousins. I like this feeling of being waited on, cared for.

It is amazing how much you can tell about a person by one simple act. *Little Man is different*, I realize, watching him, noticing how comfortable he is in the kitchen, where most boys would seem helpless. *He is not like other Zulu boys.* Someday, when he is married, he will help his wife in the kitchen. He will not always want to be waited on, just because he is a man.

The thought makes my cheeks warm, because of course, I am picturing him in *my* kitchen—nothing fancy, just a matchbox in Imbali, like we both live in now—but still, we are together.

"What are you thinking, Khosi?" he asks, handing me the drink and realizing that I've been watching him.

"Does your family throw a lot of parties?" I sip my drink, looking over the rim at him.

"No. But I *love* parties!" His eyes shine as he grins at me, my stomach fluttering the way it does before an exam.

"I'm not sure I like them," I say, thinking of the drunk man outside.

"You just haven't experienced the right kind of party," he says.

"What's there to experience?" I ask.

"A good time!"

It's true, everybody's having a good time. Except for me. Maybe

Thandi's right. Maybe I need to relax.

Men's voices, shouting and excited, filter into the kitchen where we're standing. Little Man jumps up. "It sounds like a fight," he says.

Two drunk men are talking loudly in the middle of the yard, waving their arms at each other, one of them brandishing a stick. A girl my age is standing next to them, pleading as tears roll down her cheeks. It makes me feel sick inside to see her trying to soothe them.

Little Man's brother bursts into the middle of the fight and shouts, "Calm down, my man. You, sit down." He pushes one of the men to a chair. He pushes the other towards the gate. "You, go home." As the departing man exits through the gate, Little Man's brother turns around and looks at the crowd, rolling his eyes heavenward. "Ji-sus!" he shouts.

We watch the men as they disperse, one of them leading the crying girl towards a seat.

I glance at the corner where my stalker was sitting some few minutes ago. He's gone. My eyes dart here and there, searching every corner of the yard.

I'd feel more comfortable if I knew exactly where he was.

Suddenly, I realize I'm not safe here, not with all these drunk men wandering around and fighting. Even if Little Man is with me, he can't protect me from everybody.

"I should go home," I say. "Let's find Thandi."

We walk around the house until we see her, safely cuddled in Honest's embrace. I motion to her, *Let's go*, but she shakes her head.

"I'll walk you," Little Man says, quickly. "You shouldn't go home alone."

CHAPTER TWENTY-ONE

This World and That One

"Even though you didn't stay long, thank you for coming," Little Man says as we hurry along the darkened street.

"I wouldn't have missed it," I answer.

We are only just around the bend in the street when we hear Little Man's mother calling him. "Little Man! Little Man!"

"Wait here, Khosi," Little Man says. "I'll be back."

The street is empty except for a few men smoking in the doorway of a *shabeen* somebody started in their dining room. One of them calls out, "Are you looking for a good time, little girl?"

Hurry up, Little Man, I think, hugging myself and rubbing my arms, as if it's really cold outside.

A cat darts across the road.

Is that a footstep echoing in the street behind me? I glance over my shoulder. The eerie silence fills me with a sudden sense of dread.

"Little Man? Is that you?" I call.

No answer.

There it is again. Another footstep. Every time I breathe in, I hear it—the sound of somebody shuffling behind me, a low and easy gait, somebody who has all the time in the world. A cigarette bobs in the air, glowing in the dark, a fiery spark of life.

"Who is it?" My voice is a thin wire in the dark night.

A low chuckle ricochets off the houses around me.

Sharp pang cramps sweat.

"What do you want?" My voice collapses on the final word, within the ache of that word "want." What is it that *I* want? To be left alone by all these men with their terrible desires!

Another laugh, orange sparks flying up into the black night as he takes another drag on his cigarette.

Shivering and sweating. Hot and cold all at once.

"Leave me alone," I shout. I had promised I would assert myself the next time a man tried to attack me. I had *promised*. Promised I would never feel so weak and helpless again. But now these words seem like a terribly thin defense against a man's strength, slim shreds of cloth easily ripped by nimble fingers.

All I have are my legs and this hope that I can outrun him.

So I hit the dirt, praying as I run. *Oh God, I promise I'll never go to another party if I make it home.*

My feet slip on the gravel and I fall down, breaking the fall with my hands and scrambling back up with something that feels like desperate strength.

God, please help me. I promise I'll never lie to Mama again!

And now I see him behind me, the crocodile grin, one rotten tooth in the center of his mouth.

And now I smell him, the stale stench of a man who has been drinking *utshwala* and beer since this afternoon.

And now I remember the promise he made. I'm not done with you yet, *Ntombi*. And the thing he said to me last week: I will come for you just now, *Ntombi*.

God please please please don't let him rape me.

Flashes of Little Man's image in my head. His easy grin. His dark laughing eyes. What would he *think* if I got raped? Even if he likes me now, surely he wouldn't like me then.

"I just didn't want to dance," I call back at this man who accosted me at the tuck shop, who wanted to come to my house, who wanted to *come inside*. I'm sobbing, sudden and fierce. "Please, I'm just a young girl. Don't do this."

Silence from the drunk man stalking me. But he keeps his pace up, near enough to grab me. Each time I look over my shoulder, he grins at me, like he'd reach out and grab me if he really wanted to. Or like he's waiting to do it.

In my dream where this man was chasing me through the empty streets of Imbali, it was Babamkhulu who helped me.

So I call on him now.

Babamkhulu, I know you're here. You helped me in my dream. Now I need you in real life.

The man reaches out and grabs my arm, his fingers slipping and sliding down and settling on my wrist. Fear crawls over my feet and up my legs, a snake in the darkness, slithering down my esophagus, coiling its body around the lining of the stomach.

I yank my wrist back, screaming, "Leave me alone!" My throat aching from all the tears I'm holding back. His hand, stronger than mine, as he keeps me close. "Babamkhulu! Help me!"

"I know what you want," he says, his voice low and even. "I know what you want, and I'm going to give it to you."

Hot and wet, tears spurting up, out, down my cheek. "I want you to leave me alone." My voice begging.

We're close to Thandi's house. I can see the edges of the gate, just around the corner. *Please, Babamkhulu, if I can just make it there—*

The man tugs at my wrist, winding me in towards him, crushing me up against his body, his arm wrapping around and squeezing my waist so hard it hurts. Like a crocodile, using its thick tail to press me down.

If he rapes me, God, please don't let him have HIV! I don't want to die!

Dim whispers from a voice inside my head. Or is it outside? Am I the only one who can hear it shouting? A male voice. The voice of an elderly man. *Knee him in the groin. Now.*

I jam my knee where I know it'll hurt and whirl away as he groans. Swinging Thandi's gate open, cutting the palm of my hand on the ragged edge of the gate, this other voice urging me on. *Slam it.* Run. Around the corner, behind the house. Pant breath tears.

Please don't let him follow, Babamkhulu.

I rest my head against the house, waiting. Breathing. Listening for the creak of the gate that would indicate he's entering the yard.

Drops of sweat dribbling down my forehead. Salty tears trickling into my mouth.

I wait for what feels like a long time and hear nothing. I lick the blood forming in a jagged line on my palm, the rusty nail taste filling my mouth. Glance around the corner, *quick quick*, searching for the glowing cigarette in the darkness.

Nothing but night, and a dog barking in the distance.

Please let me make it home, I pray, and that ghostly whisper assures me, *You're safe.*

Tip-toeing to the gate, I ease it open, looking left and right.

Nothing. Nothing but shadows.

I listen. Rustling as the wind blows trash across the dirt road.

Nothing. He's gone.

But as I turn to head down the hill towards home, someone reaches out and grabs me from behind.

I scream.

"Relax, Nomkhosi."

"Uncle Richard!" I'm so frightened, the only thing I can do is gasp his name.

"You see why you shouldn't be alone after dark." He twirls me around to face him. "Your grandmother was worried. She sent me after you."

"Gogo, worried?" I try to make my voice cheerful but it shakes. "She knew where I was. Why would she be worried?"

"She dreamed that Babamkhulu was shaking her awake, telling her that you needed help. She woke up shouting—she said it was so real, his hand on her face."

"That is very strange." My voice cracks. "But I'm okay."

"She's not ready for you to be gone in the evenings," he says. "And she's right. You should be home, like a good girl. I don't approve of you going out at night like this. Did you see that man lurking near the Nenes' gate? I asked him what he was doing and he just hurried away. Just think if you had tried to go home by yourself! What could have happened to you,

Khosi?"

"I didn't see him." Blood drips from my palm onto my bare leg. I clench my fist closed so that Uncle Richard doesn't see it.

"I thought you said Thandi's *baba* would walk you home."

"He wasn't there." I look back at Thandi's house, hoping there's a light on in her bedroom at least, something that will confirm my lie and make Uncle Richard believe I was telling the truth. But the entire house is dark.

"I'm glad you came to walk me home, Uncle," I say, emphasizing each word. I'm just that lucky he didn't find out I was at a party instead of at Thandi's house. "*Ngiyabonga*."

Ngiyabonga, Babamkhulu, I thank my grandfather inside my heart.

I know he saved me tonight.

CHAPTER TWENTY-TWO

Virginity Testing

The next morning when I take my bath, I'm surprised to see dark, purple bruises all over my body, like I was in a big fight.

I guess I was.

I'm still counting bruises when Auntie Phumzi arrives. Through the bathroom window, I hear Zi shrieking when she sees Auntie's youngest girls. I peek out through the open window and watch the three of them run through the yard, laughing, ignoring MaDudu, who stares at them from her front porch. Beauty's dressed in a very short white beaded skirt, her chest bare. She's wearing dozens of blue beaded necklaces that dangle between her breasts.

Oh, wow. Auntie's taking her to get her virginity tested!

I hurry into my clothes because I'm pretty sure Mama and Auntie are about to have a king-sized battle and I don't want to miss it!

Sure enough, they're arguing when I get to the dining room, where Mama is resting on the sofa.

"There is no way I would give permission for Khosi to have her virginity tested," Mama is declaring.

Her eyes flash from Auntie Phumzi to me. I start to open my mouth—*I want to go, just to see what it's like*—but she shakes her head at me.

"If you don't care about Khosi's purity, why would she care?" Auntie Phumzi asks.

"Phumzile, they're only fourteen," Mama snaps. "I don't think it encourages purity just because some old women ask girls to spread their legs so they can judge if they're still virgins or not. It's barbaric."

Auntie's voice rises in anger. "No, Elizabeth, it's our culture."

"Anyway, I expect Khosi to be a good girl, no matter what," Mama says, her voice indicating she's tired of this fight already.

"It's not just virginity testing, Auntie," Beauty says. "We sing songs about purity, and we dance, and they teach us what it means to be a wife and a mother. They teach us to respect ourselves."

Girls from school have told me all about the process: how they lay down behind four sheets, how they open their legs while an old woman inspects them. If she says they're a virgin, they get a certificate. Sometimes, they'll arrange a huge celebration, with hundreds of girls dancing and singing and celebrating their virginity.

"We sing to Nomkhubulwane, the Earth Mother," Beauty continues. "You know, she is the one who helps young girls stay pure."

"Nomkhubulwane is a pagan festival." Mama shakes her head. "This isn't for my Khosi. We are Christians."

"We are Christians, too, Auntie," Beauty says.

Auntie Phumzile looks severe. "It doesn't matter that Khosi is Christian, she is misbehaving. This virginity testing may be just the thing to set her straight."

"Misbehaving? *My* Khosi?" Mama sounds indignant.

"I didn't want to bring this up," Auntie says in a terrible voice, and now she's looking at me, and Beauty's looking at me, and their looks are accusing, "but Richard called me. He says that when he arrived at Thandi's house, it was completely dark. He doesn't think Khosi was actually there studying."

Now Gogo and Mama are watching me too. "Why would he say that?" I ask, doing my best to look completely innocent, perhaps even offended. Instead, I feel tears creeping into the corners of my eyes, my body betraying this lie.

Auntie continues. "Khosi will get into trouble with this thing of sneaking out and lying. Maybe she went to meet men. Maybe she has a boyfriend. Is that what you want?"

Nobody but Beauty notices the tears squirting out of my eyes. I wipe them away quickly and give her a shaky smile.

Mama speaks again and this time she sounds really, really angry. But she isn't angry at *me*. "Phumzile, you're my older sister and so I respect you. But this is the last time I'll say it: No. I will not send Khosi to a virginity testing. I won't have her prancing around in a little white skirt, showing off everything to every man she meets along the way." Mama flicks her hand towards Beauty and the outfit she's wearing. "You don't think *that* gives men ideas? That's too much dangerous, especially with these stupid men out there who think they can get rid of HIV if they rape a virgin."

Maybe Mama's trying to shame Auntie but all she does is make her mad. "You'll regret this, Elizabeth."

"No," Mama spits. "*You'll* regret this."

When Beauty and Auntie leave, however, Mama turns to me. "Khosi, is it true? Did you sneak out to meet men last night?"

Gogo's even quicker than me. "Shame, Elizabeth! Has Khosi ever lied to us?"

"Ehhe, you're right, Mama." Mama puts her head in her hands, like it aches. "*Ngiyaxolisa*, Khosi. We won't speak of this again."

For Mama and Gogo, the discussion is over. But I know I lied to them. I know I *did* sneak out to meet men. Well, not men exactly, but Little Man.

When Beauty and Auntie drive away, I find the little girls in the bedroom. "Let's go outside and play *sangoma*," I suggest.

The four of us sit in a circle on the cement in the front yard. I gather stones and a few sticks together. "Who wants to be the *sangoma*?" I say.

"Me, me!" Their hands shoot up in the air.

"We'll have to take turns." I turn to Zi. "You can pretend to be the *sangoma* first." I indicate the sticks and stones I've gathered. "Here are your 'bones' to throw so you can read what's wrong. Who wants to be the first patient, coming to see the *sangoma*?"

We're still playing when Little Man wanders past our yard. He jogs up to the fence and waves me to come over and talk. "Hey, Khosi!"

"You girls wait here." I let myself out of the gate and sit on a stone wall nearby. He leans against it, looking casual and soooo handsome. In just the last month, he's grown much taller than me. Now, instead of looking eye to eye, he looks down when he smiles at me.

"Where did you go last night?" he asks. "I came back thirty seconds later and *poof!* you were gone, like magic. I walked all the way to your house but I never saw you. I was so worried."

"You remember that man at the party that was giving me a hard time?"

Little Man's eyes darken. "He's been giving you a hard time for months now."

"He followed us from the party. He started chasing me." I hold out my hand to show Little Man the cut across the palm. "I barely escaped him."

Little Man is inching closer and closer, until we're almost touching, his knee close to my thigh. He reaches out and caresses my palm with his finger. Bumps spring up all over my arm. "Don't ever walk alone," he says. "It isn't safe."

"Who's going to walk with me everywhere I need to go?" I ask.

"*I* will." He sits beside me, his arm rubbing mine.

My heart is thumping so loud, they can probably hear it in Botswana. But even I know that it isn't a realistic offer. Little Man can't go with me everywhere I need to go. There are hundreds of men all over Imbali who might harm me. I read in the paper recently that one in four South African men admitted to raping a girl. Imagine that! One in four! How could anybody possibly protect me? Only God and the ancestors can keep me safe.

"Did you like the party?" he asks.

"It was too much craziness for me," I admit.

"I hope *I'm* not too much craziness for you." He leans against me, bumping my shoulder with his.

A stone is lodged in my throat. "No, you're not," I whisper. *You're perfect,* I want to add, but don't.

"Good," he whispers back.

We linger, his dreads tickling the skin on my shoulder. Even though he's looking at me, I'm too shy to do anything but stare at my feet, and then at his hands, the skin rough, the nails clean. I want to reach out and touch him. I want—

After a few minutes of warm silence, he gets up. "See you in school on Monday?"

"Of course."

His fingers touch mine to say goodbye.

I watch him walk away, my heart beating fast. When I turn around, Zi and the cousins are standing just inside the gate, giggling.

"Is that your *boyfriend*?" Zi asks.

The three of them howl with laughter.

"Shush," I say, finger to lips. "Don't you dare say anything to Gogo or Mama or Auntie." I shake my finger at the two little cousins, knowing Zi will always keep my secrets. "That goes for you two as well."

"We won't say anything," the littlest one assures me. "We don't tell Mama about Beauty's boyfriend."

"*Your* boyfriend is so *good-looking*," the other one sighs.

I look back at the corner where he disappeared. "Yes, he is," I say. "But the best part is that he's really, really nice."

CHAPTER TWENTY-THREE

COUGHING

That night, when she thinks nobody hears her, Mama coughs into her pillow, trying to muffle the noise.

I lie in bed beside her, my eyes closed, pretending to sleep.

She coughs so long, it seems like she's going to cough out one of her lungs.

Very early in the morning, I wake up and creep out of the bedroom so I don't wake her.

I go to the bathroom and turn on the light. The tub is full of pink water and smells like bleach. A white pillowcase floats inside the water. I look at it closely. The bloodstains are almost gone, bleached out. Mama is trying to hide it but she can't: they're still there, faint marks. A testimony to her night-long coughing vigil.

Once again, I'm keeping secrets: I don't tell Gogo about the bloody pillowcase in the bathtub.

PART THREE

THIS THING CALLED THE FUTURE

CHAPTER TWENTY-FOUR

SLAP

We are all worried about Mama but we don't talk about it until the afternoon before Mama is supposed to go back to Greytown.

Auntie Phumzi comes for Sunday lunch. While scrubbing the dishes, I step out the back door with a pan of dirty water. Auntie and Mama are huddled around the side of the house, deep in conversation. I pause.

"Richard says you haven't been to see a doctor." That's Auntie.

Mama: "I'm too tired to wait in line all day."

"I can send Beauty with you to the clinic, or you can take Khosi," Auntie says. "It's simple to solve this thing. It's not a problem at all."

"I'll think about it," Mama promises.

I'm afraid to move. If they hear me, they'll stop talking. I look down at the dirty water, the bits of food floating in it. My eyes scan the horizon of houses in Imbali. Looking up, I notice for the first time that somebody has climbed the billboard and spray painted graffiti on it. STOP AIDS NOW is scrawled across the bottom.

"Elizabeth, you can't just think about it," Auntie persists. "We can see all the way through to the ancestors in the other world when we look at you, you have gotten *that* thin. We'll arrange everything. You *must* go see the doctor."

"Oh, Phumzi, I don't *want* to go." A muted wail in her voice.

"Why wouldn't you want to get the advice you need to get well?"

"I'm frightened," Mama whispers.

"Frightened?" Auntie's voice sounds harsh, loud, in contrast to Mama's whisper. "They have medicine, even for the disease of these days, if that's what you have. These medicines can help you live longer, Elizabeth. And you must think of your girls."

"But what if it's too late, Phumzi? What if I'm already too sick?"

Auntie is silent for some few seconds. Then she says, "You can't know that unless you go and see the doctor."

"I don't want to be weak, Sisi, but I *am* weak," Mama admits. "I don't want to hear what the doctor will say."

I look down at the pan of water I'm carrying and suddenly understand something: this is a conversation I shouldn't be hearing. Gogo would say it's wrong to spy on somebody else's shame.

Easing the back door open, I tiptoe inside and set the pan of dirty water by the door. I'll throw it out in some few minutes, when Auntie is gone and Mama has come inside.

Gogo starts weeping that night when I begin to gather Mama's things together for her return trip to Greytown. She hides her face from us, wiping away the tears with the edge of her skirt.

"What is it?" Mama asks.

"You're too much sick, Elizabeth," Gogo sobs. "I don't think you should return just now."

Mama takes a deep breath. "Well, I'm not returning just now," she says.

I stop what I'm doing—placing Mama's clean clothes in the little bag she uses to carry them back and forth from Greytown.

"I told the school I won't be returning," she says.

"But Mama, how we will live?" I ask. Gogo has a small government pension but it's not enough to cover all our expenses. What about school uniforms? Clothing? Medical bills?

"I've already spoken to Phumzi and Richard about it," Mama says, firm now. "And we don't need to worry. They will sacrifice and help us."

"What does this mean, Elizabeth?" Gogo demands. "Have you quit your job?"

"No, Mama, I've only taken some time off so I can get well." She smooths invisible wrinkles in the bedspread.

"What are you going to do with your time off?" I ask, thinking of her conversation with Auntie Phumzi. "Are you going to go to the doctor?"

"No!" she says. "I just need to rest. I want to sleep and sleep and sleep and sleep."

Gogo and Zi and I all look at each other, not at Mama.

Mama notices immediately. "I don't want to go anywhere or see anybody," she says, her voice extra-firm. "Except family."

"But what about my birthday?" Zi has tears in her voice. "We always go to Baba's on my birthday."

Mama sighs. "Of course we'll go," she says, but she sounds so so tired when she says it.

Gogo stands to her feet, slowly, looking older than she did some few minutes before. "Let us allow your mother some rest." She holds out her hand to Zi, and we leave the bedroom.

Gogo may have silenced herself then, but this is not something she can keep quiet about for long. The next few days, she walks around the house, grumbling about Mama.

"But will she go see a doctor?" she asks the television while Mama and Zi watch our soapies—*Generations*, *Isidingo*, and *The Bold and the Beautiful*.

"But will she take the medicine that the *sangoma* gave her to take?" she asks the picture of Babamkhulu that rests on the mantle next to the television.

"But will she even go to the priest, who loves her as his own child, and ask him to pray for her?" This last one is addressed to the broom, which I'm pushing back and forth in my hands as I sweep the kitchen floor.

Finally, Gogo complains to Auntie Phumzi and Auntie joins the chorus of voices: "Elizabeth, you should go." Gogo urges Beauty to beg her Auntie Elizabeth to go to the doctor and Beauty tries: "Auntie, we'll be so much happier if we know you have the medicines you need to get well." When Uncle Richard comes home from Durban for the weekend, Gogo moans until Uncle is tired and says, "Sisi, listen to our mother and go!"

She grumbles until Mama says, "All-right, all-right! I'll visit the clinic Monday. Nomkhosi, you'll need to stay home from school and go with me."

"I have exams," I say.

"*Hawu!* Exams? You see, she has exams, I cannot go." Mama smiles, knowing what's coming next.

"But will she call the school and see if they will excuse Khosi from her exams?" Gogo asks the refrigerator.

"I'll call, I'll call just now!" Mama starts to laugh but her laughter turns into coughing. She coughs and coughs into her hand, like she's never going to stop. When she draws her fist away, there's a trickle of blood at the corner of her mouth.

I reach out to wipe it off but Mama slaps my hand away. "Don't touch it," she snaps.

I look at Mama, at my hand, then at Gogo. Mama has never slapped me before. Never. Gogo has never raised a hand to me. Even Baba has never beaten me and that's what so many *babas* do!

"What did I do?" My voice comes out strangled and high like I'm going to start crying. I can't stand the sound of it! "I didn't do anything!"

She starts to reach out to me, but I'm already running out the door and down the street, not even pausing to notice MaDudu, standing in her yard and shaking her fist at me.

I look back once and see Mama standing at our gate, her dress sagging off her thin body. She shouldn't look so vulnerable. She should be strong and brave, and when I run away, she should be able to catch me and make me behave. That's what mothers do.

Wiping tears off my face, I run through the darkening twilight, up one dirt road and down another, past tuck shops and cell phone booths, past cars that slow down as they pass me, men leaning out to wink at me and say, "Need a ride, *Ntombi?*"

I run all the way to Little Man's house.

His mother is outside watering a small patch of vegetables, dipping a large wooden bowl into a plastic bin full of water, then scattering water across the green plants.

"*Sawubona*, Mama *ka*Little Man," I greet her, breathing hard.

She straightens up, then scans the evening. "It's too late for you to be outside alone, Nomkhosi Zulu," she says. "You should be home with your family."

"I have a question about my homework," I say. "Is Little Man home?"

She overturns the watering bowl to empty it and wipes her hands on her apron. She places the watering bowl on the cement porch near the front door. "You arrive at my door, out of breath from running all this way, because you want to know about homework?" She shakes her head. "Why didn't you just call?"

I'm glad it's almost dark, so she can't see that I've been crying.

Little Man doesn't notice either, but then he probably isn't used to girls showing up at his doorstep in tears. We stand outside his gate while I admit that I don't really have a question about my homework. "I'm just upset," I say. I glance at Little Man's mother, standing on the porch, watching us.

Little Man squints, trying to see my face better.

"Does your mother know you're here?" Little Man's mother asks.

"Noooooo," I admit. "But I'm going home just now."

"Don't you young people think about your mothers at all?" she chides me. "She must be so worried, with all the drunk men between here and your house! Walk her home, Little Man, but you better hurry back!"

"We'll stop and get a cold drink on the way," Little Man whispers, his hand hovering near my elbow.

But the drunk man is sitting outside the tuck shop.

"Let's go somewhere else, Little Man." I stop so suddenly, Little Man bumps into me.

"He won't mess with you while I'm here." His lips tickle my ear.

"But what if he does?" I worry out loud. When I turn around, our faces are just a few inches apart, his skin so close, I can feel its warmth in the cold night air. We are close enough to kiss, if we were brave enough to do it.

Little Man's eyes are dark, almost black. "You have to show him who's boss," he says, sounding just like Mama. "You can't let him get away with it."

And thankfully, the man just glances at us then looks away as we step up to the screen netting to buy a cool drink. Maybe he's too drunk to recognize me. Maybe he can't be bothered when Little Man is with me. Little Man isn't as skinny as he was some few months ago. In fact, he looks like a proper young man next to me. I can't help smiling secretly. *Take that, Thandi, with all your sugar daddies,* I think. *Before you know it, you'll be* jealous *of my friendship with Little Man.* It's true, Little Man is so handsome and tall, he is already beginning to put her older men with all their money to shame.

And anyway, as Gogo says, we all arrive Mr. Big Shot but leave Mr. Nobody. I don't care that he doesn't have any money. *I* don't have money either.

We move down the street from the tuck shop and sit on a small cement wall to split the Coca-Cola. I shiver, huddling close to Little Man's body heat—but not too close, in case somebody sees us.

"So what's wrong?" he asks. "Why'd you come running to my house, crying?"

"You noticed I was crying?"

"Of course." He reaches out and brushes my cheek. I shiver.

"Mama's sick," I say. "She won't go to the doctor but—I think she's really, really sick."

"I'm sorry," he says. "Do you think—" He doesn't finish his thought.

"I don't know." Even saying the words "I don't know" makes the whole future seem uncertain. But I guess it always was uncertain, I just didn't know it.

He takes my hand and squeezes it. His skin is rough and uneven, but warm. It doesn't solve anything or make Mama's sickness go away, but it makes me feel better.

We sit there, holding hands, as long as we dare.

"Your mother is probably wondering where you are," I say.

"She's probably fuming mad." Little Man grins. "You can see the steam rising out of her ears, like in the cartoons."

So he makes me laugh before I have to go back and face Mama.

Mama's waiting just inside the front door. I'm tired and hurt but ready now to accept it when she reaches out to embrace me.

"Anyway," she says in apology, "it's just that I don't want you to get this thing making me sick. *Uyaqonda?*"

I nod. I understand. I do. But it still stings.

That night, while we watch television, MaDudu crosses the invisible barrier she's erected between our houses. She stands on the front porch, knocking.

Gogo moves the curtain to peek outside but when she sees who it is, she lets the curtain fall and she does not move.

"I know you're in there," MaDudu calls. "I will be heard. I *will* be heard!"

"Shouldn't we answer?" I ask.

But Mama and Gogo just sit there, the dining room dark, lit only by the light from the television, which Gogo turns up loud, to mask the sound of MaDudu's constant knock.

CHAPTER TWENTY-FIVE

The Clinic

On Monday, Mama, Zi, and I wait in the queue at the clinic for a long long time. Four hours! First, we wait outside, sitting in the sun while the queue inches forward. We're surrounded by other women with children, all of us shivering in the cold winter air. Some people are too sick to wait so one of their children waits for them while they sit on the wide veranda, picking at their clothes and talking with the other patients.

I remember Gogo telling me how people would queue up to see the doctor in her village when she was a young girl. It doesn't seem like medicine has changed much in all these years.

Finally, we make it inside, where we sit in plastic chairs. There's nothing but white walls, posters, and other patients crowded in here. Everybody is quiet as they wait but the silence feels like an enormous conversation in my head, everybody shouting all at once.

A woman sitting opposite us looks like a famine victim, the kind you see on television. She is just as skinny as those starving people and her lips are cracked and bleeding, eyes empty. A little girl sits on the floor beside her, staring at the rest of us with wide, black eyes.

It makes me wish we were still waiting outside.

"*Hawu*, it's as if they think the sick have nothing better to do than wait to see a doctor," I joke, to keep the tears from spilling over.

Zi sits on my lap. I stroke her plaits until she twists her head away. "Only Mama can touch my hair," she reminds me, so Mama starts to fiddle with her plaits, absent-minded.

We wait in silence until Zi asks, "When will it be your turn, Mama? We've been waiting forever!"

"The nurse told me they would call me just now," Mama says, her eyes twinkling.

We all start to laugh. "Just now" can mean anything the person wants it to mean: seconds from now or next week or even next year.

Finally they call Mama's name. I stand up, shaking Zi off my lap, but Mama shakes her head. "You two wait out here."

When she disappears into the back rooms, I notice that all the women in the room are watching us.

"Come here, Zi." When Zi sits on my lap, I nuzzle her neck, smelling the mixture of soap from her bath and dust from playing outside earlier. Such a normal, little girl smell, nothing like the sickness hovering in the air all around us, whispering in my ear, whispering, whispering.

I hear the whispers but I can't distinguish any words.

Mama stays inside for a long time, so long that I take Zi outside to wait in the sun. It's warmer there. And there's something else. As soon as I get away from all the sick people, that whispering stops.

Mama's eyes are red when she comes outside but she smiles, opening her arms for a hug. "There's my Khosi and my Zi," she says.

"What's wrong with you?" I ask, as I put my arms around her. I'm as tall as she is now, and our chests bump awkwardly when we try to hug.

"Tuberculosis," she replies as we pass through the gate to leave the clinic.

She's lying, I think, and then wonder where that thought came from.

Later that week, Mama returns to the clinic for some prescriptions and to take a class about the medicine the doctor has prescribed. When she gets home, Mama shows us the pills she must swallow, morning and night.

Zi's impressed with the different colors. "Look at the blue pills," she squeals. She starts to count them. There are so many, she loses count.

CHAPTER TWENTY-SIX

THE DAY MAMA GREW UP

Little Man calls Gogo's cell phone that afternoon to find out why I was absent from school. He offers to bring me the homework we're supposed to do in the classes we share.

"That would be great," I say. Actually, Mama called and I already have the homework, but I'm not going to tell Little Man that!

Gogo is suspicious. "Who is this guy, that he is calling for you here at home?" she asks.

"He's just a friend from school." I look anxiously at Mama. I don't want to upset her so that she starts coughing and can't stop.

"Then be friends just at school," Gogo says. She looks triumphant, like she's won some battle.

Mama arranges her blankets so that there's room for me on the bed. She pats a spot for me so I come over and sit down.

"Who is this friend?" she asks.

"It's just Little Man Ncobo," I say, thinking this is exactly why my friends like to have their own cell phones, so they don't have to face all these questions from their families.

"Little Man Ncobo," Mama murmurs, looking thoughtful.

"See? You've known him forever," I say. "There's no need to worry."

When Little Man arrives, MaDudu shouts at him not to visit our house. "They are liars and cheats there," she yells. "Are you also a liar and cheat?"

"She is just a crazy old woman and we don't know what to do about her," I tell him as I usher him inside. My cheeks are burning hot. I hope Little Man doesn't believe what she says and that he doesn't go home and tell his mother what our neighbor lady said.

"Trouble seems to follow you," he says, but he smiles as he says it.

Gogo insists that he sit down on the sofa. Then she bustles about making tea and bringing biscuits.

"I'm sorry about all the fuss," I whisper as soon as she's left the room.

"At least I get some free biscuits," he jokes.

He looks around the dining room. It must look similar to his, crowded with a sofa and a table and a television, the tile floor chipped from too many people tromping over it every day. Because he's not Catholic, I don't imagine he has a huge crucifix hanging on the wall over the television, but I'm sure he has a picture of Jesus somewhere in the living room, like almost everybody I know.

He points at Babamkhulu's photo on the mantle. "Your grandfather?"

I nod. "He died the same day I was born," I say. "Gogo has always said that means he watches out for me in a special way."

"Spooky." Little Man fakes a shiver.

"I think it's cool." I lower my voice to a whisper. "Remember how that drunk man attacked me the day of your party?"

Little Man leans forward to hear me. He glances left and right and, seeing that neither Gogo nor Mama are standing in the doorway watching us, he takes my hand.

My heart starts beating faster. He is so good-looking! I can't stop looking at his blue-black skin and his white teeth. I forget all about what I was telling him.

"Yeah?" he prompts me.

Oh, right. I was telling a story. "I think it was my *babamkhulu* that rescued me, that got me safely home."

"What about God?" Little Man has a look on his face like Mama's when she talks about these things. But I know he's not challenging me because even as he says it, he takes his thumb and rubs the palm of my hand gently, sending goose bumps up and down my arms.

"Yes, of course, God rescued me," I agree. "But don't you think God works through the people here on earth? Both the living and the dead?"

Little Man shakes his head. "It's the dead part that gets to me. Oh, my family, we believe in the ancestors, too. But it's so opposite to what we're taught in school—you know, that there's no such thing as ghosts."

"I have trouble reconciling it all too," I admit. "Especially because Mama thinks it's all superstition. But you can't prove God either. And I know what I've seen."

"Nobody can argue with that," Little Man says.

After Little Man leaves, Mama calls me to the bedroom. She pats the bed and I sit beside her.

"Just how good of a friend is this Little Man?" she asks, kneading the blanket between her fingers.

"We're nothing but friends." I'm not lying. But I'm not telling the whole truth either.

She's silent. And then she smiles. "I never told you that Little Man's father was my special friend when I was growing up, did I?"

"No!"

"Long before I met your father, he and I were—" She starts coughing, putting her face in the blood-stained towel she keeps beside her pillow. When she finishes, there are bright red drops of new blood and phlegm on the towel.

Mama won't let any of us touch it. No matter how sick she is, she insists on cleaning it herself. I hear her dragging herself out of the bed in the middle of the night. As she cleans the towel in the bathroom, she coughs even more.

Sometimes in the morning, there are drops of dried blood on the tiles. I wipe it up and don't say a word to anybody, even Gogo.

"We were sweethearts," Mama gasps, finally controlling the cough.

"Elizabeth," Gogo says, "I'm sure you can tell Khosi this story another time."

But Mama so rarely talks about the past, if I don't take advantage of it when she does, I lose the opportunity. "Where was Baba?" I ask, prompting her to continue.

"Baba had already joined the Struggle," she says. "He was living in

Mozambique."

"So did you love Little Man's father?" I ask.

"I never had the time to find out."

"Why not?"

"At the time, we were at war here in Imbali," she says. "We weren't just fighting the whites, you see. We blacks were fighting each other too. Little Man's father belonged to one side, and there were people we knew who belonged to the other side. They threatened to necklace him so he fled to Johannesburg."

"What's necklacing?" I ask.

"Necklacing was something we blacks did to each other," Mama replies. "They would douse a tire with gasoline, place it around a person's neck, and light it on fire. Many, many died that way during our fight against apartheid."

I draw in my breath, sharp. "But why? Why would we kill other Africans? Weren't we fighting the whites for freedom? So we could have the right to vote?" My voice is low so Zi, watching TV in the other room, doesn't hear.

Mama sighs. "It was complicated. When you are fighting for something you really want, everything you believe about right and wrong gets all mixed up." Mama's warm brown eyes turn dark and wet. She wipes her hand against her wrinkled skin, her face that used to be so smooth until she lost all that weight.

She looks...*guilty*. Why would Mama look guilty?

"Were you involved in that war here in Imbali, Mama?" I ask.

"*Mina? Cha!*" She shakes her head. "I had Richard and Phumzi on one side and Little Man's father, my sweetheart, on the other side. So I kept my head low. My family knew what I believed but we didn't talk about it here at home. I was afraid. You see, even family members were turning against each other."

"But Phumzi and Richard would never do anything to hurt you, Mama," I say.

"In those days, we were uncertain about many things," she says. Then she adds, "Today, we are uncertain about many things also."

Her eyes still look troubled. It bothers me to see her looking like she has many things on her mind that she can never share. But what can I do? A daughter doesn't question her mother.

"Did you ever see a necklacing, Mama?"

"*Yebo, impela*," Mama says. "You know that big house on the top of the hill?"

That's the house where the witch lives. Of course I know it.

"During a night of riots, some people took that woman's son outside and set fire to him just as the sun was setting. *Hawu*, Khosi, how he screamed—like a baby. I had to go inside to escape the smell."

I have a vision of a man crouching low in the dirt, flames streaming off his body and leaping towards the sky. "That's terrible."

"It smelled like chicken." Mama shakes her head. "I couldn't eat for days."

That little detail is the most shocking thing.

"That was the day I grew up," she says. "Before that, I thought we might really see *ubuntu* triumph. I believed that our common humanity would bring us back together. Then—I wasn't so sure, when I saw this thing."

I wonder if that's what caused that woman to turn to evil too. If she had been a good woman before, and saw what people—her neighbors, her friends—did to her son, maybe it propelled her into witchcraft, to get revenge. That is why people turn to witchcraft, because of their deep anger at others.

"Do you think the world's a better place now?" I ask. "Now that apartheid's dead? Now that we have democracy?"

"Yes!" Mama exclaims. "You have so many opportunities that I never had."

"But what about this thing of AIDS?" I ask. "It's killing so many people—" I break off, mid-sentence, seeing the look on Mama's face.

And suddenly, I know the truth. I knew it all along, of course. But it has just been confirmed. *AIDS*. That's what Mama has. The shock of it is so strong, it feels like a small fire has been lit deep in my belly, flames licking up my esophagus. It's burning me up. But no, it's not me that is burning up from the inside out. It's Mama. Her body, utterly betraying her.

"Mama," I say, helpless. It's all I can say, like I've been reduced to babytalk, with only one word in my vocabulary. "Mama."

But Mama is fierce, glaring at me. So I shut up.

"You see, you do have a better world," she continues, as if I had said nothing. "You can study science or business or medicine."

She sees the look on my face. She sees how I don't have words to answer her. How can the world be a better place when it holds such an evil disease in it?

"Don't look at the past, Khosi," she says, reaching out a soft hand to caress my face. "It's there and will always be there and there is nothing you can do to change it. Now, *now* you must look ahead. There is only this thing called the future."

CHAPTER TWENTY-SEVEN

Zi's Birthday

We go to Durban to see Baba for Zi's birthday. We'll stay overnight, then return the next day. Auntie Phumzi comes to stay with Gogo while we're gone so she won't be alone and so that somebody will be there to fix meals for Uncle Richard, who's visiting.

"Somebody needs to take care of the man," she fusses when she arrives.

Beauty and I smile at each other. We both know who will really do most of the cooking while Auntie sits around and chats with Gogo!

I'm glad to escape Imbali, even if it's just overnight. As soon as we get on the taxi, I can feel myself relaxing. No more drunk old man! No more next-door neighbor!

I sigh as I spread out in the back seat with Mama and Zi. Mama watches me with a curious look on her face. Maybe she wants to ask me why I sighed, but Zi takes the conversation in another direction.

"Mama, are you married to Baba?" she asks.

"No, Zi," Mama says. "Your Baba has never been able to afford to pay *lobolo* so we could marry." She doesn't get into the politics of it, how she doesn't want to be *lobala*-ed, how she doesn't want to be *owned*.

"So is Zulu your last name or Baba's last name?" Zi asks.

"Zulu is Baba's last name," I say. "You know that." I don't mention that, traditionally, we would not take Baba's last name until or unless he paid *lobolo*. Technically, we don't belong to Baba's side of the family at all. But Mama has always done things a little differently and so we have Baba's last name.

Zi takes this all in. Then she announces, "If you're not married, then I don't want Baba's last name. I'm not Zi Zulu anymore."

"If you're not Zi Zulu, who are you then?" Mama asks.

"I'm just Zi," she says.

Mama teases her. "Should we start calling you 'Just Zi'?"

Zi smiles and takes Mama's hand. "What's your last name, Mama?"

"Mahlasela, Just Zi."

"Why can't I be Zi Mahlasela?"

"Your *baba* loves you very much, Just Zi," Mama says. "And your sister's last name is Zulu, isn't it, Khosi? Don't you want to share your sister's last name? Don't you want to be Khosi and Zi Zulu, together always?"

Zi nods.

"Besides," Mama says, "Zi Zulu is a much better name than Zi Mahlasela!"

"Zi Zulu sounds like a rock star," I add.

"I could be famous?" she asks, squirming in the seat next to us.

Mama and I smile over her head.

Baba meets us at the taxi rank when we arrive. He is shocked to see Mama so changed. "Elizabeth, you're sick," he says.

I wish I could have warned him, but how was I supposed to tell him that Mama looks like she is dying of the disease of these days without asking whether he is also sick with this thing?

Baba starts to speak, questions spilling off his tongue, but Mama shushes him. "Can we talk about it later?"

"No, you look terrible," he says. "I want to know what's going on *now* now."

As we walk home, Zi and I run ahead, but I can hear the two of them arguing behind us. Mama looks so tired, her brown skin turning to ashes.

Gogo Zulu stares at Mama, hard and deep. "Come in, come in and sit down," she fusses. "You look terribly tired after your long trip, Elizabeth."

"*Impela, ngikhathele kakhulu,*" Mama says, sinking down into the sofa, her eyes red-rimmed with fatigue. "Thank you, Mama."

"Do you feel well?"

"Well enough," Mama says.

Zi and I sit next to Mama on the sofa, Zi cuddling against Mama and staring at Baba, suddenly shy.

"Zinhle, have you forgotten your own *baba*?" Baba asks her.

Zi shakes her head but she scoots even closer to Mama.

Baba's house is just like ours. It's small and square, with four rooms. Though Baba has no money, his brothers have been able to help his mother quite a lot and her house is nicer than ours. Gogo Zulu likes her things very nice, very proper, all lace and silk and white. She's embroidered dozens of stiff white doilies, which cover everything in the house—the coffee table; the back of the sofa; the wardrobe where she keeps her clothes.

There are even two large stiff doilies on top of the television. Zi accidentally knocks one down when she turns it on so we can watch *Generations*. She looks up—*oops*—until Baba starts to laugh.

"You'll grow up to be just like me," Baba says. "I always knock everything down too. I'm like a great big lumbering elephant in your grandmother's tiny house."

Whenever we come to town, Gogo Zulu cooks a feast. She *braais* chicken *and* beef. She cooks pumpkin, beans, rice. She's even made *utshwala*, which she brings out in a pot for Baba to drink. He lets me taste it. It tastes sour and grainy and yeasty and it leaves a small layer of foam on my upper lip.

"Albert," Mama says, "she's only fourteen." She reaches out to wipe the foam off my upper lip.

"I'll be fifteen in some few months," I say.

"Izzit?" she says and then raises a new objection. "Girls are not supposed to drink *utshwala*."

"Mama, you're always telling me I can do whatever the boys do, if I want it badly enough," I point out.

Baba jumps in on my side. "Elizabeth, are you really telling your daughter that she's not allowed to do something the boys do all the time?"

Then everybody laughs—Mama, Baba, even Zi who doesn't know

why she's laughing.

I've heard Mama and Baba fighting about this. He thinks we should be like all the other girls. He's worried that we will never get married if she fills us with ideas that are not the Zulu way.

Baba starts telling Mama about his new plan to make money. He's going to open a small stand in the Durban market and make a business selling little things, whatever he can find or buy for cheap and then sell for a small profit. "Maybe I can sell herbs," he says, getting excited now. There's almost a look of glee in his face. "I'll open a Zulu chemist! Everybody needs medicine these days."

Mama sighs. Baba is always making a plan but he never follows through. "Do you know how many people sell herbs in that market?"

He nods. "It's the biggest herbal market in all of Africa."

"And you think you'll make money doing something everybody is doing?" Mama scoffs.

There's a knock on the open door. A pretty young woman stands just outside, looking in. She's dressed in her Sunday best, and she stares at all of us, curious, and maybe a little bit hostile.

"One moment, one moment," Baba says, excusing himself and going outside. He closes the door behind him.

I can't help turning to look at the two of them standing out in the yard together. She looks excited, raising her arms, talking fast. Baba grabs her arm and lowers it, and now he is the one talking fast. I try hard to hear but only scattered words come through the closed door—*family* and *birthday* and *I'm sorry.*

She shakes her head and stares at the dirt. Baba touches her shoulder and she looks up at him then, face full of need and want and vulnerability. Just seeing that makes my stomach hurt.

At last, Baba comes back inside. "Sorry for the distraction," he says.

"Who was that, Albert?" Mama asks. Her face looks like a little girl's for just a minute.

"Just a neighbor with a small problem," Baba says. "I said I would help her later, when my family has left."

Mama looks like she has more questions, but Gogo Zulu nods at me.

"Khosi," she says, indicating I should bring out the food.

In the kitchen, I dish food out onto plates. Then I bring it out on trays, kneeling before each person as I offer them a plate. Baba is served first because he is a man, Gogo second because she is the oldest woman, and then Mama. Last, I bring food for Zi and myself. We sit on the floor because there are not enough chairs for all of us.

We bow our heads and Baba says grace. Then we start to eat. Zi is excited about all the good food we can't normally afford.

Mama pushes her food around on the plate. She eats hardly anything. And when Gogo Zulu asks her why she is not eating, she says, "*Ngisuthi.*" I'm full.

Perhaps that would have been enough of an explanation, but when her plate clatters to the floor, food scattering to all four corners of the room, I hold my breath. She has revealed her weakness more than even her thin body can: she couldn't even hold onto the plate!

Baba puts his own plate down. His movement is slow, deliberate. "Girls, go into the kitchen," he says. "I must talk with your mother."

Gogo Zulu stands up and motions for us to follow her into the kitchen. So we do. And then we sit there, listening to complete silence in the other room. *Why aren't they talking?*

"Why aren't they—" I start to ask but Gogo Zulu interrupts with a harsh, "*Hush now.*"

"What's wrong, Khosi?" Zi's hand finds mine. "Is Mama okay?"

And then I grow mad. If only they would talk! "Let's sing, hey?" I say, breaking into a rendition of "*Senzenina, What Have We Done?*" When Zi and Gogo join in, I finally hear Mama and Baba talking in the other room, in hushed voices.

What have we done?
Our sin is that we are black

We finish singing and in the sudden silence, Baba starts to shout, "Are you accusing me?"

Zi looks at me, scared, so I start singing "*Nkosi Sikelel' iAfrika,*" God bless Africa, to keep her occupied. But I try to overhear what they're saying in the other room.

Mama, with a begging voice: "No, I'm not accusing you. But I am telling you that there is no other way it could have happened."

Baba: "And what are you going to do about it?"

Mama: "*Angaz'*. I really don't know. What do you think I should do about it?"

"Have you told our daughters?"

"No. What should I tell them, Albert? Should I tell them that you, also, are sick with this thing?"

Silence from Baba. And suddenly I realize something: this is his fault. He's the one who made her ill, *he's* the one who gave her HIV, which means he must be going with other women, maybe even young girls. Young girls like me. Maybe he's somebody's sugar daddy. Who knows, maybe that young woman in the yard is one of his girlfriends?

"I'm taking medicine," Mama says. "Albert, you should go find out and perhaps you can slow this thing down before it eats you up." She starts to cry, which is exactly what I feel like doing.

"What are they talking about, Khosi?" Zi asks.

"*Hush*, Zi," Gogo says, at the same time that I say, "Mama's really sick."

Zi starts wailing. It sounds like somebody is dying.

"*Shhh*, it's alright, Zi," I murmur, grabbing her and pulling her into my arms. Her wailing subsides into muffled sobs.

"Khosi, help me," Gogo Zulu says. She goes to the refrigerator and pulls out a bottle of Coca-Cola. She opens the cupboard and reveals a birthday cake.

We light six candles. I take the cake and she takes the Coca-Cola and Zi and I follow her as she enters the sitting room, where Mama and Baba are sitting in grim silence now.

A quick glance at them—angry, sad, alone.

I reach out my hand to take Mama's. Zi takes her other hand. Baba joins us and we sing *Happy Birthday* to Zi.

Zi is so excited to see her presents—a doll, some pretty things to use in her hair, candy. She starts clapping her hands and it seems we forget all about Baba and Mama's fight.

But I can't forget. Even as we sing, I look around at this circle, at the five of us holding hands, Mama's hand now in Baba's, the way it *should* be all the time. Then the image of Mama and Baba, holding hands and singing, begins to dissolve. It wavers in the air in front of me, breaking up into a million pieces, until suddenly their image has disappeared inside the layer of salt filming over my eyes and making me blind.

CHAPTER TWENTY-EIGHT

PEOPLE KILL TO SURVIVE

When we come back from Durban, Mama goes straight to bed and doesn't get up for several days.

Finally, something is so wrong, we all have to acknowledge it. Even Zi knows now. But when she whispers, "What's wrong with Mama?," I shake my head.

MaDudu's anger seems to have subsided. She is no longer always in her front yard, staring at our house and shouting accusations when she sees one of us.

But you lose one problem only to gain another. The drunk man is everywhere. Zi and I start finding creative ways to avoid him when we arrive home from school. That means taking a different taxi, circling back, sneaking into our gate through the back or the front, depending on where we see him. Most days, Little Man rides with us, and then we can go the normal way. The drunk man leaves me alone if he's with us.

I don't want to burden Mama and Gogo so I make Zi promise she'll keep everything secret. It's not fair to Zi but what else can I do?

One day, riding back with Little Man, we pass a group of people gathered around something in the middle of the street. The three of us walk over to look and there's a chameleon right in the middle of the road, colored brown, the exact color of the dust that surrounds it. A man is poking at it with a stick, and a few other men are gathering large rocks and stones in a pile.

"What's going on?" I ask a woman standing next to me, her baby tied around her back with a bright blue and red blanket.

"They're going to kill it," she says.

This is one thing Zi doesn't need to see. "Come on, let's go," I say.

"Why are they going to kill it?" Zi asks as we walk away, kicking up dust with her feet.

I look down at her, realizing for the first time in weeks how neglected she looks. Her black eyes are huge in her face, which suddenly seems hollow, like she isn't eating enough. And her hair, which Mama had fixed last month, is starting to get ratty again. I reach out and put my arm around her shoulders, curling my fingers around to smooth it, but she shrugs me off.

"They're going to kill it because Zulus hate chameleons," I say.

"Why?" Zi looks surprised.

We pass a *sangoma's* apprentice, wrapped in a bright red cloth, her face smeared with white paste. She keeps her head down, avoiding our gaze, since during her training, she's supposed to keep herself pure, separate from other people.

"Hasn't Gogo ever told you that old folk tale about how God commanded Chameleon to tell the people they would live forever? And because the Chameleon was so slow, God got mad and sent the Lizard to tell the people they would die. And that's why people die—because the Chameleon didn't run fast enough to tell the people God's first message."

"My *gogo* has told me that story, too." Little Man meets my eyes over Zi's head and we smile at each other.

"I still don't understand why they would *kill* it," Zi says.

We've reached home. Little Man says goodbye even as Zi runs through the yard and bangs through the door. "Mama! Mama!" I hear her calling.

"I'll see you tomorrow," I tell Little Man, and run after her.

Zi is already sitting beside Mama's bed, holding Mama's hand and chattering like a little monkey in a tree. "And they were going to *kill* the chameleon, Mama, with sticks and stones," she babbles. "Isn't that terrible?"

Mama is sitting upright in bed, drinking water from a small plastic cup. "People have been killing the chameleon for thousands of years," she says, shrugging. "It's just part of the harshness of life in South Africa."

I look at Mama in surprise. She sees me glancing her way. "I'm simply telling the truth, Khosi," she says.

"But the chameleon is just an innocent animal," I say. "It's not the same thing as killing a poisonous snake, which might harm you."

"They're frightened of its magic, that it can change color," she says.

"Shouldn't we do something to stop them?" Zi asks.

"What should we do?" Mama asks. "How can we stop people from doing what they will do?"

I'm shocked by her attitude. "But killing is wrong."

"The lion kills the eland because it is hungry," Mama says. "The human kills the lion because it is frightened it will be the lion's next meal. How is it wrong?"

"But there's no point to killing the chameleon," I say. "Nobody eats it. And it doesn't harm anyone."

"I am just saying that people kill to survive."

"People do a lot of things to survive," I say. "That doesn't make it right."

"I would do what I had to, for you and Zi," Mama says. "I would do whatever it took to make sure you survived."

"You wouldn't kill," I say.

"To defend you, yes, I would." I am surprised at the firmness in her voice.

"But you wouldn't steal." I'm whispering, thinking about our neighbor's accusations.

Mama sets the plastic cup by the side of the bed and Zi knocks it over. I grab a towel and begin mopping up the water while I wait for Mama's response.

"To put bread on the table, yes, I would," Mama says. "I would not—could not—let you starve."

I hand the sopping wet towel to Gogo, trying to hold back tears.

Gogo, too, looks upset. She holds the towel and water drips on the floor. "But how is it you would rather steal than trust in God to provide?"

she asks.

"We blacks have been trusting in God since the missionaries arrived," Mama says. "And we have starved and been beaten and enslaved—all in the *name* of God. I do not believe God wishes us to preserve our morality only to make us starve to death. How is that right?"

Gogo motions to usher me and Zi out of the bedroom. "You should rest, Elizabeth," she says. "You don't know what you're saying."

As we huddle outside the bedroom door, she whispers, "Your mama is not herself..."

But I think about what she said. I understand what she is saying. God is important. He is the most important. He is the head. He's like Baba. He loves me, but he is too far away to really help in anything day-to-day. And though I pray to him, I do not really expect his help.

But I do not agree with her that it is okay to steal or to kill. It is like this sickness has invaded her mind and is eating up the mama I know and love.

CHAPTER TWENTY-NINE

CONFRONTATION

Some few days later, MaDudu is outside when Zi and I leave for school, sweeping her yard, staring at our house, muttering under her breath. A *sangoma* stands in the yard with her, watching us.

Mama has told me that, no matter what MaDudu says, I'm supposed to be respectful, so I call out *"Sanibona"* to greet them and nudge Zi until she, also, says, *"Sanibona!"*

The last few times I've done this, MaDudu has ignored me. But this time, she and the strange *sangoma* step over to the fence separating our houses.

Zi hides behind me. I put my arm out in front of her, like I can protect her.

"Ninjani?" I whisper, my voice getting softer as they come close.

"We are well," MaDudu spits at me. She grips the fence with one hand.

The *sangoma* moves to stand beside her, her red beaded plaits clanking together. One of her eyes is clouded over with cataracts. She gazes at me with her one good eye.

My chest tightens. It's the witch, the one who threatened me. Now I wish I could be Zi, with somebody older protecting *me* from this woman.

"What are you doing here?" I ask. There's a noise in my ears, way back—ocean waves far, far in the distance.

"Is that any way to greet an old woman?" she asks. "I've come to see you, Nomkhosi Zulu. I've come to see how you and your family are doing." And she laughs.

I can't meet her eyes. What will I see if I look? Will I see my own death? Will I remember something better left forgotten? Will my eyes lock on some evil, until I'm unable to turn my head away, until it eats me alive, like a fire consuming a house from the inside out?

I focus on the beaded earrings dangling from her earlobes, noticing the oval-shaped shadow hovering just above her headscarf, like she has bad spirits about her. She grins at me through the fence, her gold front tooth glinting in the sunlight.

"Haven't you seen me in your dreams?" she asks.

"*Hapana*, absolutely not," I say, feeling some small desperation to convince her. Does this mean she's sending me the dreams, and not the ancestors?

"*Hhayi*," the *sangoma* exclaims. "I never thought the child would lie."

"It's my experience that this family always lies," MaDudu says, her face flushing. "Liars and thieves, all of them." Her eyes narrow.

The *sangoma* whirls back around to face me. "*I've* seen *you* in your dreams, Nomkhosi." Her words escape through a tight grin. "We've met there before. Someday soon, we'll meet there again and you will never leave the dream. You'll be locked in there with me, forever."

My heart beats sudden hot. The whispering in my ears is becoming a furious roar, shouts of confusion and fear.

Zi tugs at my hand, urgent. "Khosi, come on, let's go to school."

I shake Zi's hand off and carefully control my voice. "You aren't in my dreams. And you never will be." My voice cracks on the last word.

And now our eyes finally meet through the wire fence. "Oh!" I cry out, hand flying to my mouth as I see the evil leaping up and out of her eyes and coming towards me. Coming *for* me.

My tongue, like a lizard's, flicking in and out, wetting my lips. Hand. Sweat. Heat.

She knows I know. She steps away from the fence, smiling, satisfied.

"What? What? What?" MaDudu swivels her head from the witch to me and back again, her words a sharp staccato. "What are you talking about? I invited you over to help me with my problem and now you are talking about dreams?"

My mouth, so firmly shut before, is wide open. "Run, Zi," I say. "Now." When she doesn't move, I shout, "*Now* now."

Zi's whole body shakes behind me but still she doesn't move. Even though I want her to go where she's safe, I'm glad I don't have to face this evil woman alone.

The witch is enjoying herself now, malicious because I've revealed my fear.

A voice emerges out of the cacophony of whispers. Babamkhulu's voice. *She's playing games with you. You must be smarter and stronger than she is.*

"No matter what I have seen in my dreams," I say, determined to sever our connection in both the dream world and the real world, "I have powerful ancestors and they are on my side. I hear them speaking just now, all around us. Don't you?" And finally my voice is firm.

MaDudu is getting impatient. "What is this stupid conversation you are having? I want to know what your family did with my money." She leans forward, her eyes bulging out as she glares at me. "You tell your mother I know she stole from me. And I'll do whatever I need to do to get it back."

"My mother was just trying to help you," I protest, glancing at the witch posing as a *sangoma*. MaDudu has no idea the evil power she has unleashed on my family. Or perhaps she *does* know and that makes it all the worse.

Zi tugs on my hand. I bend down so she can whisper in my ear. "That lady is scary," she says.

It's time to go, that voice urges me.

"It's time to go," I tell Zi. Keeping my eyes on the two women, I back up, holding Zi's hand. We back up all the way to the door until I can open it. Then we back up inside.

"*Hawu!*" Gogo exclaims, coming out of the kitchen. "You girls should be on the taxi already. You're going to be late."

I'm still too nervous to explain so Zi tells Gogo what happened.

"MaDudu keeps telling lies about Mama," she says.

"That next-door neighbor," Gogo frets. "I remember a time when she was my closest friend."

"It's not just that, Gogo," I say. "She had a witch with her. You know, that witch that lives in that big house at the top of the hill?"

"Witch?" Zi squeaks.

I take her hand in mine and squeeze, reassuring her, or maybe reassuring myself.

"Sho!" Gogo hurries forward while I pull aside the curtain to peek at the two women still standing by the fence, looking at our house.

"What are we going to do?" I ask.

Gogo looks older than normal, her shoulders drooping and her face sagging in fear. "I do not know," she says. "We'll go to our *sangoma*."

"When?" My voice squeaks, I'm so nervous.

"Saturday, first thing," she says. "We will go then."

Zi and I wait until MaDudu and the witch have gone back inside. Shaken, we sneak out the back door and down the side path that runs beside our house.

CHAPTER THIRTY

The Spirits are Fighting Each Other

That night, I have a nightmare that feels as real as anything that happens to me during the day. I watch as the next-door neighbor sneaks into our yard, carrying a large plastic bottle filled with mud. She creeps along the side of the house.

The contents of that bottle have been cursed and I have to stop her before she manages to place some of it on our house. But before I can rise to get out of bed, she reaches the bedroom window and rubs a long muddy streak just underneath it.

As she turns away to go back to her own place, I pass by, trying to reach out and stop her. But I'm moving so slowly, she slips right through my fingertips.

Like she's made of water.

Even as I look at the mud smeared on the wall, it changes to blood, dripping bright red onto the ground.

I wake up clutching a pillow, my heart beating, a river of dread flooding every crack and crevice of my mind. If only I could warn Mama—but even if I tried, she wouldn't believe me.

In the morning, Gogo finds a long streak of dirt rubbed on the side of our house.

"Do you think it's witchcraft *muthi?*" she asks, taking me around the corner of the house to show me.

The streak of dried mud is exactly where I saw our neighbor smear it in my dream.

I try to smother the uncontrollable noise my mouth is making but something deep inside is shrieking at me.

"What's wrong with her?" We both look at the next-door neighbor's house as I babble. "Mama was just trying to help her. If this kind of revenge is what comes of helping people, perhaps we shouldn't help people. It only results in jealousy and accusations and curses."

"Khosi, *shame!*" Gogo cries. "You cannot pass by a hut and fail to tie a knot. We must always help people when they need it."

I try to repair the damage of my thoughts. "But why should we help people if they just turn around and curse us?"

"Eh, if we have been cursed, we must do something about it," Gogo says. "I will go see the *sangoma* today. We cannot wait."

"Can I come?" I beg. She hesitates and I take advantage of it to add, "Please? School isn't as important as this."

"Elizabeth will never listen to me, her old superstitious mother," Gogo says. "You had better come so you can convince her that she needs to do something to stop this thing. She'll listen to you, her oldest daughter. We'll go when you've returned from school."

I don't think Mama will listen to me. But it's becoming clearer and clearer that our neighbor is so angry, she's employed witchcraft against us. I can't sit by and pretend like nothing has happened, just because Mama doesn't believe it has any power to hurt us.

After Mama falls asleep that night, Gogo, Zi, and I sneak outside. We walk through Imbali to the *sangoma's* house in the growing darkness of twilight. As we climb the steep street, dogs come running out to bark at us. Young people stand in groups here and there, flirting with each other. Other mothers and grandmothers greet us as we pass.

My stomach cramps as we approach the tuck shop but the old man is nowhere to be seen. The bucket he sits on is upended, rolling in the dirt.

We hurry past.

I hold Zi's hand on one side and support Gogo on the other. Gogo puffs her way up the hill, gripping my arm so hard, I'll have bruises tomorrow.

"Zi, why don't you run ahead and tell Thandi's *gogo* we're on our way?" I suggest. "I'll help Gogo up this last little bit of the road."

The apprentice is sitting in front of the rondavel, weaving a grass mat and talking with Makhosi.

"I'm not surprised to see you, Sisi," Makhosi says when we join them.

"Sho! Why not?" Gogo asks.

"I lose my appetite quite a lot when spirits are fighting," she says. "I haven't been hungry for two days. But the ancestors have not yet spoken to me about this thing. They are waiting. Perhaps they'll speak this evening." She gestures towards her hut. "Please, my friends, take your shoes off and enter."

Still out of breath, Gogo grunts and pushes Zi towards the apprentice.

Zi grasps my hand like she won't let go. She tugs until I lean down. "I want to come inside," she whispers. "Please, Khosi?"

I give Gogo a pleading look but she shakes her head. "You're too young," I tell Zi. "Here, you'll be sitting right next to the door. We won't be far."

Reluctant, she drops my hand and goes over to stand near the apprentice.

Elders go first so the *sangoma* enters. Gogo struggles with the low entrance. It is so hard for her to bend down—her knees are too swollen. She mutters, tries, straightens back up. I reach out a hand to help her but she shoves it away. Almost like Zi, wanting to do this thing for herself, asserting her independence.

Slow and rusty, she begins to lower herself. Suddenly, her knees buckle and she crashes to the ground, her legs splaying out behind her.

Tears spring to my eyes as I rush towards her.

She's breathing heavily and spittle gathers at the corners of her mouth as she quickly turns herself over, her face grey.

Walking here was too hard on her. She almost never goes this far, up such a steep hill.

"Gogo, I can go inside by myself," I say, helping her up and over to a chair by the entrance. She heaves herself onto the chair, taking deep, heavy breaths. "Stay with Zi."

So I crouch down and crawl through the entrance, joining Makhosi inside. The sweet scent of *impepho* swells and disperses throughout the entire room as it burns. The scent will linger in my plaits and school uniform. I should have thought to change before coming.

Smoke curls upwards in thin wisps while the *sangoma* arranges herself on a cloth spread on the floor towards the center of the hut. She takes out a small drum and, placing it in front of her on the cloth, begins to drum, a steady beat. Eyes closed, she hums then sings, a high-pitched melodic song with each line ending on a wail.

While she prepares herself for the ancestors to speak, I gaze around at the plastic bottles and glass jars filled with brown liquids, the animal skins strung along the walls and the dried herbs hanging from the ceiling.

She drums and drums and drums. The everlasting beat lulls me into a state close to sleep. If only I could lie down and take a nap.

But though I can hear the muffled rustles, the whispers, like the world is swirling around me and I'm about to faint, I can't understand the words. It's like the wind carries them away.

The beat echoes in my head, begins to sound like a voice speaking to me. It seems to come from the animal skins on the right.

My eyes fly open as I hear the *sangoma* gasp. She's sitting upright, one hand posed over the drum. "You are wondering if the ancestors have lifted their protection?" she asks.

"Yes," I agree.

"Let me ask them," she says.

She begins to drum again, a slow beat this time. "Everything is so murky," she says. She is staring at me so hard it makes me fear what she will see: doubt, fear, anger—so many of the things that make a person impure. "The voices of the ancestors are blurred. They are faint because there is so much fighting going on. *So much fighting.* They are all talking at once." She closes her eyes again and asks, "Is it possible—is it possible that the ancestors could be angry with one of your relatives? A female?" She asks like she doesn't want to ask but must because of what she's hearing.

"It's possible," I say, beginning to shake, a deep shaking that feels like it isn't part of my body. It's deeper than that.

"Your—your mother," she says, uncertain. "Could they be angry with her? Has she done her part honoring her ancestors?"

There is so much to honoring the ancestors—cleaning their graves, making sacrifices, and what what what. It is so expensive! Too expensive for us to afford. Anyway, even if Mama believed in the old ways, we would probably have failed in some ritual sometime, there are so many. I know we are not as faithful cleaning their graves as we should be. When was the last time? Oh, a year ago or more. That is too long.

If you do not honor the ancestors, they may lift their protection.

I bow my head, ashamed. "These days, it's difficult to do what we should," I admit. "Especially with the modern way of life." *And because of doubt,* I want to add. *My mother doesn't believe in any of this. She's never honored the ancestors. And she never will.*

Makhosi looks toward me but her eyes are downcast. "You have a very strong ancestor who watches over you, Khosi," she says. "I can see him, sitting beside you. He sits, just the way you sit now."

My skin prickles when I realize she's averting her gaze so that she doesn't look my ancestor right in the eyes. She's showing respect in the old way to one of the old ones.

"It's your grandfather on your maternal side," she says. "He is very jealous of your life and wants things to turn out well for you."

"Gogo's husband?" I ask. "Babamkhulu?"

She nods.

"He died the same day I was born," I say.

"No wonder his protection over you is so strong." She smiles.

I wonder if I should feel him next to me. But all I feel is this shaking. And this sudden fear. *Is this normal?*

"Have you ever told Thandi anything like this?" I ask.

She laughs. "Thandi? She has none of the spirits about her!"

I guess I already knew that.

"Khosi, can you hear him?" She pauses. "Listen. What is he saying?"

It's true, I hear it myself, a dim whisper as present as the air that surrounds us, a whisper from those that have passed to the other side.

I breathe it in. My *babamkhulu*. And others too. My fears stilled. Even though my family hasn't always done its part, they are still here, watching over us.

And suddenly I know the truth. "My family *has* been cursed," I say.

"*Impela*, this is also the thing I sense," she agrees. "Let us ask who has cursed you."

But I already know. "It's the next-door neighbor," I say. "She's been accusing my mother of cheating her out of some money. I've seen her with that *sangoma* who lives in the big house at the top of the hill, the one Gogo always says is a witch."

"Are you very sure your mother hasn't done this thing? That she hasn't opened up the floodgate of evil?"

"Why would she steal money?" I ask, thinking back to the conversation where Mama said she would steal if we were starving. "She has a job. We have enough food. Anyway, she's an honest woman."

"I know this, but you should not accuse anybody of witchcraft unless you catch them in the act. Have you seen your neighbor putting *muthi* anywhere near your house?"

I shake my head, but then I tell her about the dream I had and how we found the streak of mud under the bedroom window, exactly where I saw the neighbor rubbing it in my dream.

"Sho!" she exclaims. "This dream may be the proof—but it is hard to know because you have never been trained. Is there anybody else who might have a reason to be angry with your family, besides this woman?"

I stop to think about it. "You know about the witch. But there's also this man," I say. "He keeps bothering me. I don't know—Mama tried to get him to stop but it didn't work."

She closes her eyes again, listening. We both listen. Maybe it's a strange thing to do but in this little hut, with the *sangoma* beside me, it feels like the most normal thing in the world. Still, I'm not going to tell *anybody* that I hear voices. They might think I'm a freak.

Words form in my mind and I tilt my head to listen better to the chant beating its rhythm in my head: *Pur-i-fy the house. Cleanse the soul.*

Hon-or your dead and dy-ing. Heal the land.

"Gogo, I want this thing with our neighbor and with this drunk man to be over," I say. "Even if we don't have proof of witchcraft, I do know our neighbor's very angry with us. And there's the drunk man, his anger smolders so deep, I am afraid of what it will do to me if it doesn't disappear. Can't anger be a curse?"

She nods. "Yes, strife can cause disease or prevent us from healing or give us bad luck in our daily life."

"But I don't think it's just the next-door neighbor," I admit. "I keep hearing these words that I don't understand. *Purify the house. Cleanse the soul. Honor your dead and dying. Heal the land.* That's what I keep hearing, over and over, in my head." In fact, I still hear those voices whispering, even as I talk.

"Yes," she says. "I hear it too. The spirits are fighting each other— something has happened within your family to bring this on."

"You mean...this is something we've done to ourselves?" I ask.

"You've felt it." She reaches out a hand to touch me.

Holding back tears, I ask her, "What can you do to help us?"

"You and your grandmother can go through the purification. I can help your family search your hearts, to find the things that have allowed this evil to take hold of you and cause these problems, this self-doubt and the neighbor's anger and the man who keeps bothering you. We will do what we must so that you will have the ancestors' protection again."

"Purification is hard on the body," I say, wondering if Gogo has the strength to do it.

"You cannot fight an evil disease with sweet medicine," she reminds me.

I forget that I'm supposed to let the *sangoma* leave the hut first, since she's my elder. I just crawl through the entrance, popping my head out to look at Gogo. "We're going to do a purification, Gogo," I announce. "We'll start as soon as possible."

I'm glad we're going to do something to help the family. But I'm scared too. What if we find out something I'd rather not know?

CHAPTER THIRTY-ONE

Black Muthi

Mama calls on the cell phone as we walk home from the *sangoma's*. "Khosi, I woke up and Gogo isn't here. *Uyakhona nawe?*"

"She's here, Mama, but we're walking along the road and it's better if she doesn't talk just now." Gogo is breathing hard as we puff our way back down the hill. She's limping, probably because of her fall, and leaning hard on me.

"Where have you been?" she asks. "It's so late."

I can't lie to Mama. "We went to the *sangoma's*, Mama. I had a dream last night, and we found some *muthi* smeared on our house this morning. We think the next-door neighbor put a curse on us."

She is silent, then says, "Khosi, really."

"Mama, it's just because we *care*."

She sighs. "I'll see you when you get here."

And she is not happy. She yells at Gogo. "What do you think you're teaching *my daughters?*"

"They are my daughters too," Gogo says. Zi is hiding behind Gogo and peeking out at this mad Mama of ours, sitting up in bed, her hair a wild mess of clumps sticking straight up off of her head.

"You can do what you want, Mama," Mama says, "but please leave my girls out of it."

I take a deep breath. "Mama, this is something *I* want to do."

"No," she snaps.

"Mama—"

"Don't," she says, just the one word, before she starts coughing and gagging. I grab the rubbish bin we keep near the bed. Blood and saliva pool out of her mouth in long thin red and silver threads.

I never do get Mama's permission. She's just too sick, and the *sangoma* arrives early the next morning, while it's still dark, ready to begin the purification. Guilty and afraid, I make the decision to do it even though Mama disapproves. Gogo is urging me on. And I don't know what else to do to help my family.

Makhosi cuts the soles of our feet, our ankles, and the skin just behind our ears with a small razor blade, dabbing with a newspaper as blood pools near the skin. Gogo accepts cuts on her legs as well but I shake my head. I don't want scars where people can see them.

After cutting us, she rubs a mixture in each open wound. It burns at first; then it starts to itch, slow and steady, as though a small bug was crawling around under the skin.

She takes a plastic bottle from her bag, pouring a liquid mixture of grey-water and brown-black sludge into plastic cups. It contains bile, bits of gall from a slaughtered cow, herbs, perhaps some crocodile oil. Who knows? The contents of *muthi* are secret. Each *sangoma* concocts it with guidance from her ancestors.

We take plastic tubs and go outside.

"You need to drink all of it," she says.

It tastes like toilet water and rotten meat. I start heaving as soon as the first few drops hit my lips.

"Force it down, Khosi," Gogo urges.

Gagging at the thought of the taste, I plug my nose and drink the entire glass in one swallow. Then I puke into the blue bucket, all the liquid coming back up with the same taste as it went down but mixed with breakfast.

"There are five days of this?" I mutter.

"Yes," the *sangoma* says. "Five days of black *muthi* to purge you from evil, followed by five days of red *muthi*, to get rid of the last bits of evil clinging to you. Then you'll take white *muthi*, to replace the evil with good."

"Two weeks? It's going to kill me!" I joke.

Gogo and Makhosi just look at me.

"Sorry," I say.

Gogo is so weak after she purges herself that I help her to the door and inside *i-dining*, where she sits on the sofa by the television. Makhosi follows us and I offer her another chair. The two of them sit, talking quietly, while I go into the kitchen to boil some water and bring them tea.

As for me, I feel a sense of power and energy, like we're going to beat this thing, this curse, even that we might find some luck to carry us through these sad days.

After Gogo and Makhosi have had their tea, I walk Makhosi home. Zi zooms out the door to join us on the walk. "Why don't you run ahead and make dogs bark at us?" I suggest. So Zi runs ahead, weaving back and forth across the dirt road, creating a big noise at all the houses we pass, dogs barking and children yelling.

"When I received my call to be a healer, I think I had as many years as you now have," Makhosi says as soon as I close the gate behind us, "although we did not celebrate birthdays the way you young folk do now." She laughs. "I do not even know how old I am, can you believe it?"

I study her face, the way her jaw juts out, the way wrinkled skin sags around her eyes and mouth. It's a beautiful face, so old and kind. "Gogo doesn't know her birthday either," I say. "That's why we celebrate in October, because she likes the Spring."

"That sounds like your grandmother."

"So...you became a *sangoma* when you were my age?" I ask, keeping my eye on the road ahead, on Zi.

"I cannot say for sure, but I think I was older than you are now when I went through *ukuthwasa*," she says, naming the illness that a woman experiences before she becomes a *sangoma*. "I became very sick, so ill, Khosi, that language left me! People thought I was mad!"

"What did you do?"

"I left my home and started wandering in the hills. I did not know where I was going or when I would come home, I only knew I had to go.

I spent all those months hearing the voices of the ancestors and gathering herbs. Eh, one day, I wandered too close to the Thukela river and a serpent sucked me deep beneath the waters. It was no ordinary serpent, Khosi. It was one of my ancestors, coming to me in the form of a snake. I was underwater for many many months. Eh-he, I have no idea how long. Sho! it was lonely! But when I finally emerged, I knew how to honor those who went before us, the old ones who protect us from beyond the grave."

"Why do you have to go through *ukuthwasa* before you can become a *sangoma*?" I ask.

"Because you must understand sickness before you can help others through it," she says. "You must return from the place of death in order to heal."

Zi reaches the turning point and looks back to see how far behind we are. She waits until we catch up with her, then she runs ahead again. I wish I could bottle her energy and sell it as *muthi*. I wish I could give some of it to Mama.

"Thank you for telling me your story," I say.

"You will have your own story, Khosi."

"What do you mean?"

She reaches out and touches my shoulder. "The calling on you is strong," she says. "I think you're meant to be a healer."

"Mama would never give her blessing." I feel like I'm confessing something. The truth is, I want to be a *sangoma*. I want to help people in the old ways. Even if Mama doesn't like it.

"If the spirits call you, you'll know it," she says. Then she adds a warning. "But if they call you, you must follow them, otherwise, you can die."

My limbs begin to tremble, faint at first, then stronger until Makhosi notices that I'm shaking.

She examines me while I struggle to control myself. Then she asks something unexpected. "What do you plan to do to your next-door neighbor?"

The question surprises me. "Nothing."

"You don't plan to take revenge for her curse? You don't want to hurt her back?"

This feels like a test. I hope I pass.

"Gogo and I are seeking protection from the ancestors," I say. "I'll let them deal with our neighbor."

She nods. "Good," she says. "And if you found out that your mother had really done this thing, stolen money, what would you do?"

"But Mama would never do that," I protest.

"I'm sure you're right," she says. "But that's not what I asked."

Ever since I saw the lightning bird's wings flapping away across the cement near our back door, I've been preparing for this moment. What *would* I do if it turned out Mama was a thief?

Makhosi tilts her head to watch me, like a lizard sunning itself on a rock, its dark eager eyes seeing my every move before I see them myself.

"I don't know, Gogo," I say. "I think I would get her to return it. We don't need that kind of money."

Her wrinkled jowls relax into a smile. "There's something very good in you, *mntwana wam'*," she says. "I see it. You'll see it, too. You'll have to make some difficult choices to walk into your calling. But I'm sure you'll do what's right and good."

We've reached the Nenes' house. Zi's waiting for us beside the gate. I look at Thandi's window, wondering if she's already left for school. My normal life seems so far away right now.

"What were you talking about?" Zi asks as we head back down the dirt road.

I take her hand and think about everything swirling around in my head. "She just wanted to know how Mama's doing, that's all," I say.

Zi's face screws up with a wish she's afraid to speak. "Mama's going to get better, isn't she?" she asks.

Her hand in mine is so small and trusting. What is she going to do without Mama? What am *I* going to do? Suddenly, the only thing I want is to call Baba, ask him to come to Imbali, ask him to take care of us. But Baba's sick, too. He just hasn't faced it yet.

"Everything will be all-right, Zi, I promise." I clutch her hand. I'll take care of her, of course. I'll take care of everybody.

CHAPTER THIRTY-TWO

THE FIGHT

Mama gets upset when she sees I'm not going to school. "Not only is this foolishness," she says, "but you're missing school, too."

But she's too weak to complain much. Her lips are cracked and dry, even though I rub them with balm that the *sangoma* gives us. She lies half-in and half-out of bed all day, too feeble to get up but not wanting to admit it.

Because of the purification rituals, we're not supposed to talk to our neighbors, or hang around our friends like normal. But on Thursday, we need milk and bread, so Gogo sends me to the tuck shop.

I hurry, not looking to the right or the left, afraid to meet someone and ruin my purity. That's why I don't see Little Man until he grabs me around the waist and pulls me off the road.

"Little Man!" I gasp.

"Hey, *wena* Khosi!" He grins.

His fingers linger on my hip for some few seconds before he withdraws his hand.

I'm that glad to see him, I smile back and let it all shine through my eyes, all the feelings I have for him.

And his eyes are shining with the same gladness.

"Where have you been, Khosi?" he asks, reaching out his hand to touch mine. "I look for you every day in school. You've been gone all week. Are you sick?"

He moves his hand from my fingers to my forehead, like he's my mother, checking for a fever.

"My mother is really ill," I say in a low voice, looking around to see if anyone can hear me.

"I'm sorry," he says, suddenly sober. "Is she going to get better?"

We've been a house of lies ever since Mama got sick. But I can't lie to Little Man. "I don't know," I say.

We start walking back to my house, shuffling through the dust. I notice how dirty his feet are in his flip-flops but they don't bother me. Is this what love does to you? It's mad to think some guy's dirty feet are the most beautiful thing you've ever seen but that is exactly what I'm thinking.

"Is that why you haven't been in school?" he asks. "Are you taking care of your mother?"

Should I trust him? I ask myself. Then I think, *Of course. It's Little Man.* So I ignore all the *sangoma's* warnings about keeping this thing secret.

"We're doing a purification with the *sangoma*," I say.

"Who, your *gogo* and your mama?"

"Me, too," I say.

"You're taking *muthi* every day? Purging? Praying?"

"Every day."

"Do you really think it'll work?"

"It has to!"

He shakes his dreads, like he's disappointed in me. "You're the smartest girl I know. Why did you let your family suck you into this superstition?"

I choke back sudden tears. Did I make a mistake telling him?

"You sound like Mama!" I say.

"Why don't you just take her to a doctor?" he asks. "They can really help her!"

"Doctors don't know *everything!*" Now I feel defensive. I glance at his feet, which were so beautiful some few minutes ago. Now they just look dirty.

"Well, they know more about disease than some stupid old *sangoma*."

"Whatever happened to 'it can't hurt and it might help,'" I say, reminding him of our conversation a couple months ago.

"I meant in addition to doctors," he says. "I only meant if doctors had *failed*."

"Well, this *is* in addition to doctors!" I'm suddenly angry. "Doctors can't help her anymore. And this isn't about my mother's sickness, anyway. This is about things *doctors* don't know anything *about*."

"Hey, Khosi," he says, shocked and starting to back away, "I'm sorry!"

But it's too late. I don't want to hear all his blah-blahs of apologies. I don't know where all the love I felt for him went or what what what but it is *gone*.

What does he know? What would he say if he knew that I keep hearing voices in my head? Would he say I was crazy? Would he tell me I must be imagining things? Would he tell me *I'm* just like those stupid old *sangomas*?

"Don't tell me we're not helping her when you don't know *anything* about it." My voice rises to a shout, almost a scream. Just before I take off running, I find myself yelling, "And don't come running after me with stupid explanations or excuses. Just leave me *alone!*"

I'm glad my house is close. I reach it, panting, and look back. I already regret that I told him to leave me alone. I'm hoping he's followed.

But the street behind me is empty.

CHAPTER THIRTY-THREE

RED MUTHI

A week passes. I stay in the house, afraid to go outside and meet anyone again. Now that my anger is gone, I just feel hurt. Sometimes I look out the window, hoping that Little Man will be outside, lingering, but either he never comes or I never look out the window at the right time.

I even break the ban on socializing and call Thandi.

"How's it?" I ask, hoping she'll bring up the topic herself so I can tell her about the fight and ask her to find out if Little Man is really angry with me. Maybe he's said something about it at school. If he has, Thandi will be the first to tell me.

But Thandi's preoccupied. "I haven't seen Honest in a week," she says, bursting into tears. "Do you think it's over with him?"

"How would I know?" I ask. "Did you fight?"

"Nooooo," she says, so slowly I know she's lying.

I don't really want to talk about her fight with Honest. It's a whole different level than my fight with Little Man. So I make up an excuse. Another lie. "Oh, my *gogo* is calling me," I say, and hang up.

Gogo and I go to the backyard every morning with our mixture of nasty-tasting *muthi*. The red *muthi* tastes even worse than the black.

Shivering in the cold, we down the pot of liquid and purge in the big blue buckets that I leave outside. Then Gogo limps back inside while I wash the buckets.

Mama gets sicker. Sometimes she just lies in bed and doesn't move all day. Her lips look like a butcher came and cut them all up with a long knife. The sores on her back weep until her sheets are soaked. Sometimes they dry to her skin and then I have to peel them off, listening as she quietly sobs.

I don't notice the stench unless I've been gone for some time and I return home. Then I realize that our house is beginning to smell like the carcass of an animal, rotting on the side of the road.

She's wasting away.

And Gogo's weak too. She sleeps more now than ever before. Even during the day, she naps inside near Mama's bed.

Yet she seems content.

I'm the opposite. All the time, I hear those whispers, and they're still saying the same thing: *purify purify purify.* It's becoming an urgent chant in my head, and even my worry about the fight I had with Little Man recedes in the face of that word. Over and over and over. *Purify purify purify.*

But that's what we're doing! I shout at the voices in my head.

Purify purify purify, they shout in response.

And then there are the dreams. Every night.

In one dream, I see the gold-toothed *sangoma* watching as Gogo and I purge the red *muthi.* Instead of vomit, a snake slithers out of my mouth as I bend over the blue bucket. She cackles as she watches and I wonder if her medicine is so powerful, it's blocking ours.

In another dream, I see Mama standing in a long queue, waiting to see God. The queue is made up of all the people that need healing. I float up above the queue, up up up, above the earth, until I can see how it stretches all the way around the earth's perimeter, coiling and winding and twisting from China to Europe to America. It's a giant serpent, swallowing the globe.

"The purification isn't working," I tell Gogo.

But Gogo refuses to stop. "First we have to complete it," she says. "Then we'll see if it is working or not."

"That's not what I meant," I say. I try to explain, but I don't have words. "I think there's something *else* we need to be doing."

"Hush, Khosi," Gogo snaps. "You bite and soothe like a mouse."

She doesn't understand. She can't hear the voices whispering in my head.

"It's not working," I tell Auntie Phumzi.

"Don't let doubt stop you now," she says.

So we keep going, even though I'm beginning to feel like anyone can look at me and see right through me.

Mama stays in bed all the time now. Nothing changes. In fact, the only thing that changes is where I sleep. Each night, I make up a bed for myself in the dining room on the sofa. In the morning, I fold the sheet and blanket and put them, with my pillow, back in the bedroom.

For the first time in my life when Mama's in town, I'm sleeping alone.

CHAPTER THIRTY-FOUR

PROMISES

It feels like I've started to puke blood and guts every time I purge. There's a small itch in my chest. And a raw feeling in my throat, like I've swallowed boiling liquid. Raging sores dot my tongue, the insides of my mouth.

I'm beginning to feel like I am all emptied out of everything. All I'm doing is the next thing and then the next thing after that.

Is this how Mama feels?

Strange things have started to happen. I feel this strong sense that somebody is watching me, that I'm being tested. Sometimes, dizzy after we expel *muthi* into the bucket, those dim, distant voices break through the fog and roar like lions.

Clearly, yes, the ancestors are trying to give me a message. And I'm sure, whatever it is, it's important. But I have no idea what they're saying anymore.

I'm just hoping for something to happen that makes me feel whole again.

"You're losing weight, Khosi," Auntie Phumzi observes while we're standing at the foot of Mama's bed.

Mama is so sick now, she doesn't even *try* to clean her own bloody cloths. We put them in a big tub with bleach and let them soak for a long time before we clean them, just in case.

We've moved everybody out of the room—even Gogo and Zi are sleeping in the dining room with me. I'm the strongest, so I help Mama during the night. Auntie Phumzi comes during the day so I can get a little rest. I haven't gone to school in two weeks. What's going to happen to my studies? My good grades in biology? And if my grades go down, will I lose my scholarship? I try not to think about it.

Mama starts to speak through her cracked lips. She has almost no voice, so we have to lean in to hear her. "You need to stop," she whispers.

"Mama, today was the last day of *muthi*," I protest but even as I speak, my voice gives out, just like Mama's, cracks and breaks and bleeds. "The only thing left is a feast for the ancestors."

"The expense," Mama moans.

"How do you feel?" Auntie asks, looking at me with concern. She looks in my face, puts her hand on my forehead. "Khosi, you're burning up! Are you well?"

Mama suddenly sits up, then falls back on the pillows because she is too weak to sustain herself. "I don't like this," she murmurs. "You *must* stop it."

"I'm fine," I insist, my voice hoarse and deep. "It's not the *muthi*, I promise, Mama." I've never before felt my vocal chords but now each word I speak feels like I'm pushing on a blister deep inside my throat. "*Angiguli*. I just feel a little weak, that's all, not sick."

Mama grabs my hand as I start to walk out. "Khosi," she whispers. "I want to tell you something."

My stomach hurts as I sit on the bed beside her. She wipes her mouth off with the back of her hand, then reaches under the blankets and brings out a sheaf of wrinkled papers, clutching them in her hand. "I've been saving money since you were just a baby," she says, still coughing.

"Mama, do I need to hear this just now?"

"Yes," she says. "I need to tell you before it's too late."

She shoves the papers towards me, thrusts them in my lap. "This money, it's not much but it's enough to pay your school fees at university if you're careful. So you can go to college."

I glance down at the papers in my lap. "That's so many years away."

"Keep them someplace safe," she says. "Don't tell anyone about the money. If you tell anyone, they'll want to use it. We always need money for this, for that, for nothing, sho!" She shakes her head. "It's better if they don't know about this thing, hey, Khosi?"

"Where is this money?" I ask.

"It's in a bank account in Pietermaritzburg," she says. "Those papers have all the account information. It's in your name. Nobody can withdraw that money but you. Nobody."

"Why, Mama? Why are you giving this to me now?" I already know the answer but I want to hear her say it. *Mama, please talk to me.*

She ignores the question. "You like biology," she says. "Become a nurse. If you become a nurse, you'll always have a job."

"What, practicing medicine with this thing of HIV running around our country like elephants that have gone crazy?" Yes, I'm mad. I don't even bother to keep the anger out of my voice. I've never spoken like this to Mama. Of course, I'm not angry at her. Or maybe I am. Yes, I guess I am. Why did she wait so long before she went to see the doctor, and here she is, urging me to go into medicine? "That sounds like a death sentence, Mama! It's only a matter of time before—"

"No, no, you mustn't stay here in South Africa," she says. "As a nurse, you can go to England. You can take Zi with you and escape this place."

"I don't want to go to England!" I protest. "Everybody I love is *here*."

But Mama has it all planned out. "Hush, Khosi," she says. "It's a good place to live. You can go to England and escape this thing of AIDS."

"You want me to leave Gogo?" I ask.

"Yes!" she cries. "Leave before the whole country goes up in flames, before everybody dies of this thing, before only the old people and the children are left."

"But I love South Africa," I say. "I want to help my country."

"You think I don't love South Africa?" she asks, and the tears roll down her sunken black cheeks, once so fat and round and lovely. "I've lived here all my life and I'll die here without ever leaving. But you and Zi can escape if you're smart and get training that they need in England. Hey, Khosi? Hey?"

"Let me think about it," I say, the words sour in my mouth.

"Promise me you won't tell anybody about the money," she insists, and her voice is urgent now. "They'll want to use it for my funeral, to make a feast for the ancestors. They'll spend *all* of it on my death. They'll waste it honoring me and sending me to the other side when the best way to honor me is to use it for your education. Promise me you'll keep it a secret, Khosi."

What else can I say? I break down, crying. "I'll keep it secret, Mama."

"You won't spend a single *rand* on making a feast for me after I die," she says.

"No," I sob.

"And you'll become a nurse," she prompts.

I've never thought about becoming a nurse. But now it feels like this is the one thing Mama's asking me, like I'm making a death-bed promise while she grips my hand. "Yes, Mama."

"I see a healing gift in you, Khosi," she says.

"If I have some kind of healing gift, why can't I help *you?*" I cry. "That's all I want. To see you well again. That's it. Nothing else. Anyway, why do you think I'm doing this stupid purification?"

"That's exactly what I mean," she says. "See, Khosi? You have a fierce desire to help people. You'll make a wonderful nurse."

I sigh, wondering if I have what it takes.

"Promise me something else, Khosi," Mama says. "Before you go to England, you won't get involved with men here."

I think about Little Man. Does he count? He's not a man...yet. "I'll try."

"As a nurse, you'll be able to pay for Zi's college," she says.

"Mama, why are you asking me all these questions? Why are you asking me to make all these promises? Are you—?" Even I can hear the pleading in my voice. I stop just short of begging to know.

And of course, Mama doesn't answer my questions, just as she hasn't talked to anybody about what is making her so sick.

Instead, she reaches out her hand, stopping before it touches me. Her hand hovers in the air. "Khosi, it's just a matter of time before Baba also—" She chokes and stops. She speaks in a very low voice. "You'll always take care of Zi, won't you?"

"Of course!" I almost shout the words. How could Mama think I wouldn't take care of Zi? I'm her second mother. She's my heart, my blood.

She relaxes back, the pillows sighing with a poof of air as she sinks into them. She looks almost peaceful now, like she's settled something in her mind, something she hasn't wanted to talk about for so long but now she's finally broken the silence.

As for me? I feel like a ghost, wandering through the house, not even sure anymore what is real and what is a dream.

CHAPTER THIRTY-FIVE

WANDERING

I try to embrace what Mama has told me. I try to understand it. I try to pretend that the nagging doubts aren't there.

But they are.

I lie down on the sofa, closing my eyes, trying to get rid of a headache. Gogo sits beside me, rubbing my forehead with her soft, wrinkled hands.

"Gogo," I say, keeping my eyes closed, "you need to call the priest."

"For what, Khosi?" she asks. I can hear the worry in her voice, and I can interpret it easily. She thinks something is wrong with me.

"For Mama," I say. "He needs to come to our house to see Mama."

Gogo's voice drops to a whisper. "I can't tell the priest we are doing this thing of purification."

"He doesn't need to know," I say. "But Mama needs to give confession."

Through a haze of sleepiness and waves of pain in my head, I hear Gogo on the phone, chattering in rapid Zulu, inviting the priest to come. Rolling over so my face is to the sofa's back, I let my body sink into sleep.

I stagger to the bathroom, the voices in my head thumping and throbbing. Passing the bedroom, I peek through the open crack. Mama is inside, murmuring, her voice low. The priest, Baba Mkhize, is kneeling at her bedside, holding her hand.

I stumble back to the sofa and lay there until I see the priest come back into the dining room. Even though I feel terrible, I sit up to greet him.

"*Sawubona*, Baba," I say.

"*Yebo*, Khosi." The look in his eyes. Sad and thoughtful. Like he knows more than he should know about the world, and about my mother, and about this family.

Gogo hobbles out of the kitchen. "Baba, Khosi isn't well," she says. "Can you pray for her?"

He kneels beside my head, withdrawing a small jug of holy water and a small jar of anointed oil from his pants pocket. He sprinkles me with water and makes the sign of the cross with oil on my forehead.

"We pray that you will heal this little one, in the name of the Father, the Son, and the Holy Ghost," he murmurs.

For just a minute, the babbling in my head ceases. Reaching out my hand to touch his, I look at him, the questions in my eyes, wondering what Mama told him, wondering what I need to know.

"Shhh, Khosi," he says. "God forgives. And I know you will do the right thing."

My head bumps back into the pillows as he leaves. I close my eyes to an image of Gogo's large hips as she disappears back into the kitchen.

Thandi comes over. Her right eye is bruised and puffy, and she has scabs and ugly bruises on her neck and arms. She sits beside me on the sofa in the sitting room and begins to whisper her story to me. "You can't tell anyone."

"You're in trouble," I murmur, but it feels like my voice is coming out of my body from far away, like I'm speaking from the kitchen or even farther, from the back yard, almost like the voice isn't mine, just an echo I hear speaking in my head.

"Yes, but not like that," she says and then she starts to cry.

Her story comes through in pieces, broken apart in the fog that separates us, then reassembled together in a way that doesn't make sense. Something about falling pregnant, Honest, and a love potion.

"Wait, wait," I say. The weight of her words is pressing me down. I lie back on the sofa. "Let me get this story again."

"It didn't work, that's what I'm telling you," she sobs. "I told Honest I had fallen pregnant and asked if he thought he could get *lobolo* so we could marry, not immediately but in some few years. He just laughed because he's already got a wife. So I went to get a love potion. I thought he might leave his wife if he really loved me."

"Where did you get a love potion? From your grandmother?"

"No, no, Gogo doesn't make love potions. I went to one of her friends, another *sangoma*. But now Honest claims it wasn't a love potion at all—that I made him sick instead, that I poisoned him."

"So he beat you," I say, pointing to her face.

She nods and begins to weep again.

"Honest is sick?"

"Yes."

"You should go to the clinic," I say, crawling into that place of sleep that seems overwhelming. "You need to find out the truth."

"Oh, but Khosi, I'm so afraid," she wails. "He thinks his problem is the love potion, but what if they tell me I have this thing of AIDS?"

"You should find out before it's too late, before you get sick."

"I'd rather not know," Thandi says. Her words come at me slow and thick.

I don't have the heart to send her into Mama's room, to say, *Look, see what comes of not getting tested? Of not getting the help you need?*

"Just go home, Thandi," I tell her. "I don't feel well."

She keeps talking and worrying but I can't listen anymore. I'm too tired. Too sick. I cover myself with a blanket and let her words float right over my head and out the door.

Some few minutes—or days—later, I stumble out the door, only a few *rands* in my pocket and an unclear destination in my mind. The city center—that's where I'm going, but I don't even know why.

My head is still pounding with the babbling of voices.

I pass MaDudu. She opens her mouth to speak, but I drift by. There is nothing she can say to me right now to compete with what I am already hearing inside my head.

I pass the drunk man who likes to bother me. "I haven't seen you for a long time, *Ntombi*," he grins, the teeth in his mouth shifting and rearranging until his face doesn't make sense anymore, a long snout growing out of his throat and his nose floating off near his face somewhere. "I'm coming back for you." He clicks his finger at me and winks. "Today. Just you wait for me. You'll be mine." He breathes, whispering one last lush word, "Tonight."

I brush past him like he's a fly but even as I do it, I know better. His eye winks over and over and over in front of me as I step onto a taxi. The man who takes money looks at my pale face and gestures for me to go to the back seat. The people scoot over to make room. They scoot far away, leaving me lots of space.

The man's eye winks at me. His rotten tooth wavers in the middle of his mouth, shimmering...like gold. He clicks his finger at me. He clicks his finger. He clicks.

I shake my head but the visions glisten in front of me, flickering in and out like a bad television connection. They refuse to go away.

I get off at Freedom Square. The ladies selling toys and candy wave at me. "Where's your little sister?" one of them asks as I pass.

"*Ekhaya*," I say. "At home."

I wander here and there, down arcades where clothing is heaped in piles just outside the store, people picking through, looking for just the right skirt.

The drunk man's eye winking.

The witch's gold tooth glimmering in the air, right in front of me.

I want to hit that man's eye, the witch's mouth—but it's all an illusion. I run my fingers through the vision and it breaks up. I realize there's nothing there but air.

I'm so thirsty. I ask a store owner for something to drink and she brings me cold water from her tap. I drink it and then ask for some more.

"When was the last time you had something to drink?" she asks.

I shrug. I can't remember. I can't even remember my name.

I don't know where I'm going. I don't know...I don't know where...I drift with the wind...until I'm standing in front of Standard Bank of South Africa. People are streaming in and out, like water, their faces a blur of rearranging cells and bits of dark flesh.

I push the door open and wander inside, not sure what to do now. I get into one of the queues, then stare at the tile floor as it inches forward. My heart is beating. *What am I doing? What am I doing?*

And the voices in my head, wordless, but responding to my question with a chorus of approval. My head lightens, clears.

Whatever I'm doing, it's the right thing.

I get in line and wait with everybody else.

Something snaps in place when the teller looks at me expectantly. The drunk man's winking disappears and the woman's face shines, luminous, in front of me. Who am I? Nomkhosi Zulu. What am I doing here? Finding out just how much money my mother is leaving me.

I pull out my ID. "I have a bank account here," I say. "I'm wondering how much money is in it." I'm surprised at the amount she names. "Is that enough to go to college?" I ask.

"If you're careful," she reassures me.

"How did my mother save that much money?" I ask.

"She must love you very much," she says, smiling at me.

"Yes," I say, looking at the slip of paper with the amount written on it. "I guess she does." Then I ask the question that I've been dreading to ask. "How long has she been saving money?"

The lady ruffles through the papers, looking. "She made only one deposit. It was on the 30th of March, earlier this year."

When she says this, I suddenly feel like Mama has died, even though I know she's still back in the house, spitting up blood on a cloth and sweating her way through the sores pockmarking her body.

"One deposit? What do you mean?"

The lady explains, patiently, "I mean that she put all that money, the entire amount, in the bank at the same time."

"*Hawu!*" I say. "How is that possible? That much money?"

"Maybe she saved it in her mattress for a long time," the lady jokes.

I walk out the door and down the street, not quite sure where I'm going. I sit on a bench in Freedom Square, in the center of the city, looking at the women sitting on the ground near me, their goods spread out on the blanket in front of them. I'm surrounded by people working so hard just to feed their kids. None of them had the opportunity Mama has handed to me.

I look at the paper the bank printed out for me. The amount is staggering. Enough to go to college, if I'm careful, as the woman said.

Mama told me she had been saving a long time. But she lied to me. There is no way Mama would have left that much money in the house or at her room in Greytown, not for so many years.

And if she lied to me...then...how did she get the money?

And at what cost?

I think about our next-door neighbor, all her many accusations. I think about how her husband died early this year and it was in March that Mama helped MaDudu get the money from his insurance.

Oh, Mama, what have you done?

A sudden image of her before she got sick, her face healthy and whole again, swims in front of my eyes. "I'm sorry, Khosi. I'm sorry." I hear her voice in my head again. And I see her, clear as day, before me.

Are those tears in her eyes?

Yes, Mama will weep. She'll weep when she realizes that her dreams are dead, now that I know she has done this thing. I can't use stolen money for college. I know this. And she'll weep when she realizes that her sin has opened the door of evil in our lives. I hope I can close it before it's too late.

When my taxi arrives, I just sit there. I know I need to go home but I can't face anybody yet, especially Mama. What am I going to say to her? And how am I going to say it?

I wait for a long time. I wait while the air grows damp around me and my fingers grow numb with cold and the sun starts to set and I'm shivering in my skirt.

It feels like a dream as I step inside the taxi and move to the back seat. The three women shift to make room for me.

I sit next to the window and stare at my reflection mirrored back, cracking up into a million tiny pieces, dissolving into a vision of the woman on the hill, her gold tooth shining like a tiny sun in the window's reflection. Her face, hovering like a ghost's just outside the moving vehicle. Her mouth gnarled and twisted like old tree trunks.

She's smiling.

And that's when I know.

She's come back for me. She's finally come back for me.

CHAPTER THIRTY-SIX

BATTLE

Imbali is swallowed up in darkness when the taxi spits me out in front of the tuck shop, my body hurtling like a rocket from the vehicle, the witch behind me, faster, her voice crackling in my ear. *Did you think I'd forget?*

Stumbling falling the rough gravel the stones cutting.

Blood on my hands, my knees.

And I'm staring up into another face, the cool stale beer breath stinging tears to my eyes.

"If it isn't my own little sugar girl," he croons, grabbing me by the hair, yanking me forward until I fall at his feet, a crumpled heap. "The one who wouldn't let me *come inside.*"

"She's *my* sugar girl," the witch snaps.

"Please," I beg. "I'm just a little girl. Don't do this."

The witch's hand snatches out, shoves my face in the dirt, tiny stones and soil snarling their way up my nose as I gasp for air.

"What do you want with her, anyway?" the drunk man asks. He leans over and whispers in my ear, "I'll treat you like a queen, sugar girl."

"Please," I moan. "Please leave me alone."

"I claimed her first," he tells the witch.

But she laughs, a laugh that quickly tangles up into a growl. "*You* exist because *I* created you. She belongs to me."

"We can share her then," he whispers, wanting me that bad, the starved look on his face.

I lift my head. "Let me go!"

"Shut up, stupid girl," the witch says, smashing my face back into the dirt. She grabs my arm and begins to drag me, the drunk man running alongside us, panting as he tries to keep up.

I feel dizzy, something thumping in my chest and making it hard to breathe. The echoes of the ancestors' whispers beating in rhythm with my heart. And that's when I begin to pray, to call on the ancestor whose protection is so strong—Babamkhulu.

You can't fight everybody, I say to the witch, knowing she can hear me even if I don't speak out loud.

As I pray, words dribble out of me, leaking one by one, on and on, forming a river at our feet. The witch stops, looks at the river, lets go of my arm.

Where are we? the drunk man asks, looking around at the darkness and the water, the fear in his eyes only a pale reflection of the fear he made me feel back in Imbali.

This river is the crossroads, the witch hisses, *the crossroads between life and death.* She gazes at me. *How did we get here?* Her voice, deadly.

That's when I know. *She's not the only one with power.* I'm the one who brought us to this place in the dream world.

I look across the river. The witch, the drunk man, and I are trapped on this side, surrounded by nothing but black space and nowhere to go but the river.

I look at the water, thinking I could make it to the other side if only I knew how to swim. It's true, I'm scared of water. But the push to cross the river is urgent. Slowly, I dip my toes in the water. Toes, then feet, then knees, then thighs and hips and waist, until I'm up to my breasts, suddenly panicky about going under and not knowing how to swim.

The witch grabs my arm, trying to hold me back, and I twist it to free myself from her grasp.

I'm going to leave you here in the dream world, I say.

The dream world is my world, little girl. Her face is ugly as it looms near, her body twisting, sinewy, slimy.

You'll never come back to the real world, where you hurt people.

We'll see. She slithers into the water, her face shimmery, slick like oil. She slinks under the surface.

I thrash around, wondering where I should go, when something grabs my ankle and pulls me under, sudden, forceful, and I'm face to face with the witch, flogging through the water towards me, her gigantic mouth open wide to swallow me whole.

The drunk man slips into the water, his belly suddenly scaly, his legs morphing into a strong tail, his eyes bulging, his crocodile grin becoming the long snout I saw on his face earlier.

Back in the deep, in the darkness of water and slimy plants and slithering snakes and the stalker-crocodile's sleepy-slow-sudden hunt. His hunt for *me*.

Do I have the power to overcome both a witch and her servant, a crocodile?

But Mama is going to be here, soon, crossing over into the land of the shadows, where the ancestors live. I know this as surely as I know the witch will never stop unless I teach her a lesson she doesn't want to learn, unless I show her the power of the ancestors on my side.

If Mama is coming to this place, maybe I, too, should stay here.

Perhaps I don't want to return, I say out loud. *Perhaps I want to stay here. And when the crocodile comes for me, I'll let him take me. You can't fight death.*

So I stop resisting the water or the crocodile or the snake and accept the punishment that comes.

Soft, through layers of water, a sudden splash.

My eyes fly open.

Little Man is in the water, staring at me, his eyes wide open with horror. "What are you doing, Khosi?" he shouts. "Why aren't you fighting back?"

"I'm afraid," I admit.

"So afraid you're willing to *die?*"

"If I die, at least I can be with Mama," I say, knowing suddenly that this is the place where she is going, if she isn't already here.

"But what about Zi? What about...what about me?" His voice shakes, the warm tenderness of his sobs cuddling me.

Oh.

At that sound, my body shudders and rebels, resists this fate, dying here in this watery grave.

The crocodile comes for me. I grab his mouth as he strikes, a tooth sinking into my thumb, blood spurting out. But I hold on, thrashing and kicking. Stunned, he lets me go, his powerful tail thumping against my backside as he swims away.

The witch's eyes meet mine.

She's as shocked by the power surging through my body as I am.

My breath is coming fast in short, funny spurts. Even with power, you can still be afraid.

Before she can seize on my fear and turn it against me, I threaten her. *Is this what you want? To fight until you die? Or are you going to turn around and leave too?*

Behind me, across the river, the ancestors are gathering.

The witch looks at all of us, angry, then turns around and swims away.

If you dare come back for me or for anybody I love, I will hunt you down and kill you, I shout at the sinewy figure retreating.

Sharp awareness for one painful second when I surface from the deep deep water and Auntie breathes, "She left us, Khosi, she left peacefully, saying only, 'I love you all.'"

Looking beyond her, I see the *sangoma*, her old wrinkled face looking concerned.

"Where did my mother go?" I ask.

"To the other side," she replies.

"No! She can't leave yet! *I'm not ready!*"

Slowly, I sink back into the dream world. "Sleep, Khosi," the *sangoma* says. "Sleep—but then return to us. Find your way through the water and bring your gifts of healing back to this world."

Slipping back into the world with the river, Babamkhulu, and... Mama. Mama's on the other side of the river, shouting at me. She's so far away and the river is so big. How did she get here? And why is she on the other side?

I look back across.

Mama is no longer alone. Behind her are hundreds of people—no, thousands—all of them waving at me.

"Goodbye, *mtwana wam'*, my child," Mama calls, still waving. "*Sala kahle!* Stay well!"

She turns her back and disappears into the trees on the other side of the river.

"Wait, Mama!" I call. "I'm coming! Don't go!"

Everything is black and murky around me, my legs and arms moving through thickness of water, learning to touch and identify. I'm pushing aside the watery resistance—until I see dim shapes in the water ahead of me, a sudden vision of my *babamkhulu* and oh! of Mama. She's there with me, in the water, her face restored to its beautiful roundness, her beautiful body swaying in the water.

She smiles at me. "Khosi, my child," she says, holding her hands out towards me. "Forgive me." Even in her happiness, she is weeping, knowing what she has done.

But her face is shiny again. The bruises, gone. The weeping sores—disappeared. The insistent thought, and I'm grateful: *She's been healed. She's been healed.*

And then Zi's voice, whispering my name, over and over. "Khosi. Khosi. Khosi. Khosi. Khosi."

I wave fingers towards Mama but do not touch her. It's like I'm saying goodbye but promising to return at the same time.

"You must do the right thing," Mama says, her voice now beginning to fade as I float upwards. "I'm sorry. Please forgive me..."

I know exactly what she means. "Of course, Mama. I'll take care of everything."

I look over at Babamkhulu. He nods and I nod back, knowing that I'll see him again.

Then I swim to the surface. Because Zi still needs me. I can hear it in her voice.

"What happened?" I gasp, feeling as though I've just breathed for the first time in my life, air knife-like as it thrusts through my lungs.

I open my eyes and, as I do, Zi clutches me, buries her face in my shoulder, sobbing. Stretching my arm over the sofa, I look beyond Zi to Gogo and Auntie, their faces pale; then I glance at my thumb, which throbs and aches, and notice a small puncture wound right in the center.

Gogo's face floods with color. Auntie's relaxes into all manner of peace.

"Some drunk man beat you badly, Khosi," Auntie says, tenderly.

Flashes of the drunk man's face morphing into the crocodile.

"Did he...?" My voice cracks on the words. I'm not sure I want to complete the thought. "Am I still...?"

"Your virtue is still intact," Gogo assures me.

Thank God. He didn't rape me. I'm still...safe.

"How did I get away?" I ask.

"One of your school friends found you and carried you home," Auntie says.

"He was distraught," Gogo says. "He kept saying, 'I should have protected her.'"

Gently, I feel my bruised face. My eyelids are heavy, my lips swollen and sticky. "Who was it?" I ask. "Who rescued me?" But I already know.

"Little Man Ncobo," Gogo says.

I groan, my face to the wall.

"He likes you," Zi says, her face popping up a few inches from mine. "He likes you a lot."

Gogo sighs. But in that sigh, I hear a promise. I just hope it isn't too late—that Little Man really does like me that much, like Zi says.

"The police came and took that drunk old man away," Auntie says. "He won't bother you again."

But what about the witch? Is *she* also gone for good? Did I really leave her behind, stuck in the dream world? Or has she just started playing games with me?

Whatever comes, the ancestors will protect me. That witch is not the only one with power.

CHAPTER THIRTY-SEVEN

Mama Joins the Ancestors

I wander around the house, looking at everything covered with cloth—the television, the mirrors, pictures, even the windows.

I never want to eat again.

The truth? I feel like I've lost. I no longer care what happened in the dream world. I don't care that the witch slithered away or the stalker realized I'm stronger. No matter where I wander, there's one room I must avoid: the bedroom. Mama is there. Or rather, her body is there, shrouded in a sheet, Gogo sitting beside her, mourning.

I should go inside that room, but I can't. I don't want to look at her body. I would rather remember her, waving at me happily from the other side of the river, calling out, "Stay well, my child! Stay well!" That is a much happier vision than the one I glimpse when I pass by the bedroom to go to the bathroom—the edges of the sheet, Gogo's keening, her deep breaths, the sobs.

I speak from the hallway. "Do you need anything, Gogo?"

She shakes her head. Pats the bed, inviting me to come sit beside her. It's where I should be, the oldest daughter, mourning my mama with her mama.

But I can't. I can't go in that room. "I'll be back, Gogo."

For two days, neighbor women have been making all the food for the family members and friends who are here. I'm just well enough to toddle into the kitchen and watch them as they stir sorghum in a massive pot on the stove. One lady has a pot full of *phuthu*. Watching her stir it, I stare at the white grains sticking to the wooden spoon.

"How much food are you making?" I ask.

"Enough for a thousand people!" she claims. Then she tells me what I should be doing, rather than watching her cook. "You should sit in the bedroom with your grandmother."

I drift outside where the men are roasting meat over a fire. Baba and Uncle Richard and all the other men who knew Mama throughout her life sit around the circumference, drinking *utshwala* and talking, falling silent when I approach.

Baba meets my eyes. There is something really different about him. He seems shaken, his face haggard. I notice a few white hairs in his scraggly beard and coiled through the black hairs on his head. He's getting old, my father. He's getting old and now, unless he goes to the clinic and gets help, he's going to die, sooner rather than later, and I will have lost both my parents.

The tears well up in my eyes. *I'll speak to him*, I promise. *But I can't think about it just now.*

I wander back inside to the sitting room, where many of the women, even Gogo Zulu, are gathered around Auntie. I stand there, listening to the women chatter, until Zi comes and stands right beside me, perfectly silent, fiddling with the knobs on a drawer. She doesn't look at me.

Finally I notice her hair: the tight curls knotted and matted, as if she's been neglected. Zi still hasn't learned to let any of the rest of us be her mother.

Putting my arm around her, I say, quietly, "Zi, will you let me wash and comb your hair, please?"

She's very still for a minute, even refuses to respond, but when I reach my hand over to caress her head, she doesn't jerk away like usual. She lets me work my fingers into the knots, threading through them. As my fingers dig deeper, she begins to hiccup and then to sob and finally she's quiet. But she stays near me. When I'm done, she buries her face in my stomach.

A few hours before the funeral, the men begin to look solemn and official.

The house and yard, which has been so crowded, empties as people leave to walk up the hill to our church.

"How will we possibly feed everybody at the feast afterwards?" Auntie Phumzi frets, but then she shakes her head. "It is good," she says. "Elizabeth was well-loved."

Our next door neighbor emerges from her house, sober, for once silent with her accusations.

Her children and grandchildren wait outside while she exits the gate and comes over to our yard. She calls to Auntie, "*Sawubona*, Phumzile!"

Auntie's eyes meet mine. I peek at MaDudu. She's standing at the gate, a shawl draped around her bent shoulders. She looks...penitent. Maybe she believes her curse caused Mama's death. For that, she should be ashamed. But now that I know what Mama did, I know that we're covered in shame too.

Auntie walks over. Their conversation is brief but Auntie nods and touches the old woman on the shoulder before she shuffles back out of the gate. She and her family begin the long walk up the hill to the church, to the funeral.

"What did she want?" I ask when Auntie returns.

"She said we must use her yard and home for all the people that come."

"That's kind of her," I say, knowing Auntie has no idea what I really mean. "Gogo's missed her friendship."

"Perhaps her anger is gone now," Auntie says. "Death is the greatest force for forgiveness."

"Yes," I agree, wondering if I can forgive Mama myself.

Finally, it's our time to go. Men load Mama into a wooden coffin and place it in the back of a van we've borrowed for the day. Gogo and Gogo Zulu get into the van. Gogo calls out to Zi, "Come, child, come with us," and Zi runs over to climb into the van.

There's no room for the rest of us. Auntie is driving her car but it's already full too. So Baba and I are left to wait until she comes back to pick us up.

I want to be angry at Baba, for what he did to Mama. But all I can think is how he will leave us too, unless he goes to the doctor *now* now to get help. "How's your business, Baba?" I ask. But what I really want to ask is this: *How are you feeling? Are you well? When will you die, Baba?*

"Oh, it's getting started that's so difficult," he says.

Will it ever happen, Baba? Will you ever get started? And how will it ever happen if you're sick?

"I tell you what I would really like to do," he confides. "I would really like to sell some things that make *muthi* and the other things that *sangomas* need to do their business. That is what I would like..." His voice trails off. Then he adds, "But I don't have the money to make a business."

I want to offer some few *rand*s to help him, to take some money from the bank account so he can make his business. But it isn't my money to give. Instead, I offer a smile and again I promise myself that I will talk to him when all this is over.

When we reach the church, it's filled with people—neighbors and relatives singing hymns, clapping hands, waiting for the funeral to begin. They struggle to get the coffin out of the back end of the van, and the people part so we can pass. Zi runs over to take my hand. We follow Gogo and Gogo Zulu inside, after Uncle Richard, Baba, and the other men carrying Mama's coffin shoulder their way through.

We follow them up the aisle towards the front of the church. I look out at the sea of faces, at people I don't recognize. Baba Mkhize, the priest, is standing at the front, waiting for us, waiting to begin.

And then I see Little Man. He's sitting a few rows behind Auntie Phumzi.

My eyes move from Little Man to his mother, sitting next to him, and then to his father, who looks like he's swallowed something bad and it hurts his stomach.

Little Man looks like his father, his face solemn as he watches me. He gives me the slightest nod, like he's encouraging me, like he's saying I really can do this. Like maybe he's saying he's sorry.

MaDudu sits in the back, her head bowed, ashamed. Soon, I will have to go to her and tell her about the money. Give it all back to her. *I'll do it,* I promise. But that is a task for another day—another task I can't think about just now.

I sink deep into my own thoughts, so deep that I don't remember the service. I don't remember the songs we sing or the words the priest speaks or how many people press money into Gogo's hand afterwards, a tradition that will help us pay for the feast and for all the food we've been feeding the people who came the last days to mourn Mama's death.

Zi sits through the service, holding my hand and glancing up at me for reassurance every few minutes, the way she once did with Mama. I hold her hand and I sing hymns and I listen to the priest, his words drifting over me like clouds in the sky. Here, but gone so quickly. I think about all that Gogo and I did to purify our family, and what I found out because of it. I wish Mama was still here. I wish I could talk to her about stealing the money. I wish I could cry.

By the time it's over, my lips feel like they're bleeding.

CHAPTER THIRTY-EIGHT

MAKING UP

A few days after the funeral, Gogo looks out the window and sees Little Man lingering by the gate. "Khosi! Khosi!" she calls. "Your friend is here, outside the gate!"

I glance in the mirror in the bathroom—wow, my face is still so swollen—even as she yells, "Khosi, *shesha!* He's leaving!"

It's true, he's about to turn and walk away. "Little Man!" I yell, fumbling my way out of house.

He turns around, quick quick, and grabs the gate. "Khosi," he says, sounding so glad to see me that relieved little tears spurt to my eyes. "Come talk to me."

I let myself out of the gate and we walk down the dirt road. He holds my elbow with his bony hand. "When are you coming back to school?" he asks.

"Next week."

"Thank God," he jokes. "All these girls keep bothering me, and I keep telling them, 'Khosi Zulu's coming back to school. She's my girl and if you don't leave me alone, you better watch out 'cuz she's one tough girl.'"

The way he says "tough girl," it feels like he's caressing me, his voice low and intimate. It's confusing. There was our fight, and now here he is, and things are back to normal, except everything's changed. Everything. Everything except my feelings for him.

"I miss school," I say. "What are you studying in biology?"

"The life cycle of the malaria parasite," he says. "Boring."

"It sounds interesting to me. And important. Do you know how many Africans die of malaria each year?"

He laughs. "Yes, they told us. Almost a million!"

"Malaria is not as bad as AIDS," I say, "but they say it kills more people than AIDS in the long run."

"You really do like science, don't you?"

"I'd like to go to college and study biology," I admit, "but my family doesn't have the money."

"Sis man," he says, "haven't you heard of scholarships?"

Scholarships. No, I hadn't thought of that. All I'd been thinking about was the money Mama stole, the money I still need to give back.

"Do you really think I could win a scholarship?" I ask.

"They have a lot of scholarships for black students these days," he says. "And you're the smartest girl *I* know."

The way he says that makes me feel shy. "Thanks."

He elbows me. "Come on, let me see where the *sangoma* cut you."

"Didn't you say I was stupid for doing the purification?" I ask.

"Ah *wena*," he says. "I told my mother what you said and she told me I'm the stupid one. Maybe you can forget about it."

I tilt my head until he can see the slits where Makhosi cut me behind the ears with her knife. They are already slender long scars, barely visible.

He touches them. I shiver.

"That's nothing like the bruises I have from that man's beating," I say.

"I know." His fingers move to the bruises on my face. They're healing but still visible. His touch is light. Loving, maybe.

"Thanks for coming to my rescue," I say.

He shrugs, hand dropping to his lap. "All I did was carry you home."

"Maybe you saved my life."

He grins. "Then you owe me."

I go along with the game. "What exactly do I owe you, Little Man?"

"A kiss?"

My breath comes out in a sudden whoosh. "I'd like that," I whisper, "but not here. All the houses have eyes."

We both look around us at the innocent looking matchboxes on all sides. He touches my hand. "You're right. But I'll hold you to it."

"I better go inside before Gogo gets suspicious," I say. "Before she starts complaining that I'm out here with a boy."

"What are you talking about? Your *gogo* loves me now."

I laugh. "You're right, she does. If I hadn't come out to say hi to you, she would have come out herself. But how did you know?"

"She came to my house while you were still sick. She said your whole family is in my debt." He grins. "I think we can be friends now and she won't care."

After I go inside, I open the door to peek out, to see if Little Man is still out there. He sees me watching him and this foolish grin breaks out all over his face. He waves at me, then takes off, running down the road.

I watch him until he completely disappears.

CHAPTER THIRTY-NINE

Dreams Are Our Eyes

"Sibongile Nene was here this morning," Gogo says a few days later, twisting a cloth around her old hands as she speaks, nervous or excited or both. "She says your sickness was *ukuthwasa*. She said she believes you will be a particularly powerful *sangoma*, if you would like to become one. She would like to train you."

My head jerks upright.

Ever since I knew Mama was sick, was sick for real, was sick beyond healing—I knew this was coming.

Or perhaps I knew when I saw Mama and all the ancestors behind her on the other side of the river, perhaps then I knew that this was coming.

Certainly, ever since the ancestors came to stand behind me until the witch slithered away, I knew that I had received the call.

And when I walk outside and up the hill and see that witch who attacked me—reduced to mumbling in her yard, gazing at the trees and the skies but looking like she never sees anything at all—every time, I know what I'm supposed to do.

"She said to tell you, 'Dreams are our eyes,'" Gogo says. "She said you would understand."

What I want to say is difficult. "I want to do it," I say, the words slow to come. "But Mama wanted me to be a nurse. And I promised I would try." I do want to be a *sangoma*. But that's such a different world than the world of nursing.

"Why not?" Gogo responds, quickly. She looks disappointed for a second, then says, "You can do anything you want." She rubs her eyes, tired suddenly. "I don't know how we'll afford it," she adds. "But we will manage something. Phumzi, your uncles..."

"I'll study hard and get a scholarship," I say, thinking of what Little Man told me. "Besides, becoming a *sangoma* is expensive, too."

"For you, Sibongile said she would do the training for love." Gogo lifted her hands, palms up, to show me they're empty. "We would need to make a feast at the end—that's all."

I start to speak, but instead begin to cry.

"What's wrong?" Gogo asks.

"It is just that I—I miss Mama so much." I'm overwhelmed by the sudden emotion of it. The vision I had of her in the water, beautiful and whole again, with God and with our ancestors, is beginning to fade. Over time, will it disappear?

I remember the way I jumped in the river to get to the other side, to join the ancestors, to join Mama—even though I didn't know how to swim, I wanted to be there. How tempting it would have been to stay there forever, with Mama and Babamkhulu.

But I'm here, not there. And I have a lot of difficult decisions to make.

"Oh, Khosi, your mama has become one of the ancestors," Gogo says. "You can still turn to her for help."

But I keep wondering about that. Can you become an ancestor if you've done something really wicked here on earth?

I hope Gogo isn't looking out the window when I let myself into the Dudus' yard. I don't want her to ask questions later. This errand is private. But I'm sure Mama, up in heaven, is glad to see me doing it.

I knock on the door and enter when I hear, "*Ngena.*"

MaDudu is alone, sitting on her sofa in a dining room that looks almost exactly like ours except we have a newer sofa and a bigger TV. She starts to rise when I enter, then she sits back down as if she's given up, the air escaping from her mouth in a low hiss.

Tears roll down her cheeks and she hides her face in her hands.

"Nkosikazi, what's the matter?" I run to her side and stroke her hand, gentle. Now that I know she was justified in her anger—even if she wasn't justified in going to a witch and cursing us—I feel tender towards her. Anyway, all those problems caused by witchcraft are gone now. Even Gogo's sore knees are better!

"I'm sorry about your mother," she says. "I'm an old woman and I don't want this anger between us anymore. Can we just live in peace?"

"I didn't come to fight you," I say. And because I'm holding back all the tears of these last few months, I hiccup.

Then I open my bag so she can see all the *rands* inside, not all of the money in my bank account but what they would allow me to take out in one withdrawal. I thrust it at her, not wanting to see it again, just wanting to get it off my hands and go home.

"It's yours," I say. "It's all yours."

"What? Where did you get it?" she wails, and in her voice, I can hear all the suffering she did these months since her husband died.

Oh, Mama. Why did you do it?

"It was in a secret bank account," I admit, hoping she'll stop asking questions so I can leave and we can get back to our normal interactions as neighbors, just saying hello, being kind, nothing between us.

She goes as silent and still as Mama did when she first accused Mama of stealing her money.

"I didn't know," I whisper. "I didn't know until just a few days before my mother died."

She looks up and our eyes meet and I know she understands.

"Shhh," she says. "We won't speak badly of someone who's gone to the ancestors."

"Gogo doesn't know," I say. "Nobody knows except for me. Please?" I know I don't have the right to ask her to keep it between us but I hope she will.

"Shh, shhhshhshhh," she says again, and I understand that she won't say a word. This secret is between us.

I begin to weep. All those pent up tears. I weep and weep, kneeling beside her, until she puts her hand on the back of my head.

"*Ngiyabonga.*" I thank her.

"I'm so ashamed," she says, bowing her head. "I'm ashamed of all my anger."

"I'm not worried about it, Gogo," I say.

"I'm worried about it," she insists. "I've sinned against your family. It's terrible, what I've done."

I don't want her to speak these words out loud. It's better if we leave the knowledge of what she did in my dreams. I wipe my eyes with my blouse. "Anger leads us all to do things we regret."

"No, but I went out of my way to harm—"

"I understand," I say, silencing her before she confesses to witchcraft out loud, which would mean I must do something about it. "I was angry with you, too. Please forgive me."

She still hasn't taken the bag with her money in it, so I shove it at her again. "Take it, please," I say. "It's yours. And there's more coming. I just have to bring it."

Finally, she closes her hand around it and lifts it into her lap, gazing at the stacks of money inside.

We're still, a quiet that is more than two humans not speaking. The voices that have been filling my head for weeks now are at rest. At peace. They aren't gone, they're just calm. I can feel their approval in the peaceful silence.

I already know that when I need them, they'll be back.

Can I live my life now? I ask and hear my answer in the silence. Because living my life isn't about leaving all of this behind. It means embracing this, all of it. The voices. The call to be a *sangoma*. Mama's dream for me to be a nurse. MaDudu's hand resting on mine. All of it, everything.

Seeing that money disappear from my hands into MaDudu's makes me certain that I want to be a healer in *both* worlds, the world of science and the world of the ancestors.

Maybe I can do both, I think. *Maybe I can be a nurse and a* sangoma. *Maybe mixing traditional healing with medicine will really help people in a new way. It'll be hard, but I know I can do it. Why not? Who's going to tell me I can't do it in today's South Africa?*

CHAPTER FORTY

FEAR

Thandi's bruises are healed but she still hasn't gone to the clinic. At first, the excuse was Mama's funeral and this was something I could agree with. But then the days slipped by and, finally, I confront her about it.

"Really, you should go," I say. "Have you spoken with Honest?"

"I haven't seen him since that day," she mumbles.

She agrees to go if I accompany her. But, she says, we must go to a clinic far away, where nobody will know.

"Anyway, I can't do these mobile clinics," she says, "where they come and you test and by the time you leave, everybody knows if you have this thing or not."

"Have you told your family that you're pregnant?" I ask.

She shakes her head. "They'll find out soon enough."

At school, Thandi's pregnancy is the topic of conversation for everybody. Katie Green tells me her father would *kill* her if he found out she was pregnant.

"Really?" I ask. "Thandi's young, but I don't think her family will be angry."

"Why not?" she asks.

"At least, she's able to have children," Little Man jumps in to explain. "That's the most important thing."

"I don't know if I even *want* children," Katie says.

I've never heard of such a thing before. How could you not want children? Having children is the most important milestone in life. "You need to meet my little sister," I say. "Then you'll want children."

She laughs. "You should meet *my* little sister. Then *you'll* change your mind!"

It feels good to laugh at her joke. But somehow, it hurts at the same time.

As we go inside the school, Little Man holds me back.

"It was lonely here while you were gone," he says.

"I missed this place too," I say.

"That's not what I meant." He looks at me full on, eyes meeting eyes. "I missed *you*."

I reach out my hand, suddenly bold, taking his and squeezing it.

He grins at me and I feel better. About everything.

Katie pokes her head out of the door where she just disappeared. She sees us holding hands. "Hey, are you two lovebirds coming or what?" she calls, mischievous.

Little Man grins at me, jubilant. Because of the "lovebirds"?

"After you," he says, opening the door and bowing slightly as he ushers me inside, just like a British gentleman.

A few days later, Thandi tells me she isn't going to go to the clinic to take the test after all. Why? Honest has come back to her!

"What about his wife?" I ask.

"He'll leave her," Thandi says.

"When?"

"He says he will and I believe him." She sounds annoyed that I don't believe him.

"Okay," I say, trying to figure out a way to convince her to go to the clinic. Making her mad won't help. "Why don't we go anyway? It's better to know."

But Thandi covers her ears with her hands as if the nurse is right there, waiting to tell her whether she has HIV. "You can go for yourself some day, Khosi," she tells me.

"If you have this thing," I say, "it'll kill you. Unless you take medicine."

"Then let it kill me," she says. "Honest came back to me, and that's what matters."

"It's too late to stop the pregnancy," I point out. "But it's not too late to—."

"I don't want to know." Thandi pushes at the air like she's pushing me away. "If I get really sick, *then* I'll go to the clinic. But even then, I'm not certain what good the knowledge would give me."

"There's medicine for it," I protest. "You don't have to give in to this thing."

"So many people we know have it," Thandi says. "What good does testing do for us? If I have it, I'll still die, whether I know it or not. If what they say is true, it is probably the thing that will kill me, the thing that will kill us all. *You* just as much as anybody, Khosi."

I'm like God in my firmness. "It won't kill me," I say.

"How can you be so sure?" Her question is almost a taunt.

But I don't need to answer Thandi. I know it's true.

I'm too young to know whether Little Man is always going to be in my life. But I do know one thing. Little Man is a good friend. He's not going to pressure me, not the way Thandi's sugar daddies do. He's too kind. And like me, I'm certain that he wants to be safe, to hold the future secure.

I've decided: I'm going to stay pure, even if it's old-fashioned.

So I already know I'll avoid HIV.

And someday, when I'm done with my studies, I'll get a good job. I'll be a *good* nurse in South Africa. Maybe I'll move to England, like Mama wanted. But whatever I do and wherever I go, I'll take Zi with me.

To protect her too.

CHAPTER FORTY-ONE

This Thing Called the Future

I'm finally ready to tell the *sangoma* my decision. Little Man, Zi, and I walk to Makhosi's house after school.

"Don't you two get into trouble while I'm inside," I tell them.

"Yes, Mama," Little Man says in a high voice, like he's a little kid. He and Zi laugh, then give each other high-fives.

I'm glad they get along so well. Gogo also loves Little Man. She says he is her grandson as surely as I am her granddaughter. Even Uncle Richard and Auntie Phumzi have accepted him.

There's a long line of people in front of the *sangoma's* hut. So many people waiting to see her, just like they wait at the medical clinic.

I slip around the side of the house to find the apprentice. She's squatting on the ground in front of a big black pot on a big fire, scattering herbs into the thick liquid. Her black skin is pasted over with thick white paint, just little bits of black peeking through, like the opposite of stars in the night sky.

"*Sawubona*," she greets me.

"*Yebo*," I reply.

"*Ninjani?*"

"*Sikhona*," I say.

She starts to stir the thick porridge in the pot. It smells like burning rubber and meat and some herbs.

"Are you here to tell Makhosi that you're going to train to become a *sangoma?*" she asks.

I nod. "What's it like, the training?"

"Sho!" she exclaims. "You must not expect to sleep. You must know that you will be working very hard."

She puts down the thick stick she's using to stir the *muthi*. "Wait here," she says. She disappears for a minute or two and then comes back and motions for me to enter the hut.

The room is smoky. Makhosi looks really tired, her eyelids thick smudges as she reaches out to squeeze my arm in greeting. "Nomkhosi Zulu," she says. "Have you come to say you will be a *sangoma*? That you will come train with me?"

"Oh, yes, Gogo," I say. I know absolutely it's the right thing to do.

She smiles at me. "Good. I'm glad. We'll begin as soon as you're ready. Tomorrow, if you like."

"Thank you."

We sit there in silence. I have another question for her, but now that I'm here, I don't know how to ask it.

"What's worrying you today?" she asks, eyes closed.

Makhosi waits and I wait. It is almost like we are listening.

There are so many things I want to ask but I have one overwhelming question, the thing that dictates my every thought right now. Do I dare ask it?

I take a deep breath and let my voice find me. If I can't trust Makhosi with these questions, who can I trust? "Do you think if someone does something really wrong here on earth, they can still make peace with what they've done once they've died?"

"Eh!" she says, her exclamation more of a breath than anything like surprise. "Why do you ask?"

"Can...can my mama become an ancestor even if she did something wrong?"

Her touch and tone are gentle. "Khosi, healing doesn't only come here, now, on this earth. It's also something for the other side."

I suddenly remember this is a Catholic belief too. Purgatory. And now I realize why we did the purification, and why we kept praying, even after we knew Mama was going to die. No matter how strong and powerful your enemy is, you keep on doing it, no matter what, because there's always hope, and if anyone has enough power to help you, it is God. Healing an illness isn't about healing the body. It's about curing the soul. And only God can do *that*.

"Life doesn't end with the separation of the spirit and the body. *Akudlozi lingay'ekhaya*," she says. "No spirit fails to go home." She reaches out and pats my hand. "The hard part, Khosi, is for those of us still living to let go of our anger towards the people who have already passed on to the other side."

I guess that means I have to learn how to forgive Mama for what she did.

Those dim voices that spoke to me, first here in the *sangoma's* hut and then when I was sick, they're babbling now. Like they're all trying to reassure me, like they're all saying we're in this together. I guess this is something I'll have to get used to if I'm going to be a *sangoma*. I'm even beginning to recognize Babamkhulu's voice through the gaggle of voices murmuring to me.

"Thank you," I say, grabbing Makhosi's hand in mine, making my promise to her with touch. This whole thing will be hard—forgiving Mama, becoming a *sangoma*, becoming a nurse, just living life—but it's what I have to do.

When I crawl out of the hut, the first thing I see is Little Man and Zi sitting on a wall outside of the gate. They're laughing so hard at something that they don't even hear me coming up to them.

Zi stops laughing and slips her hand inside Little Man's. She looks up at him, as if what she's going to say is confidential, a secret. "Do you think Mama can hear us?" she asks. "Do you think she knows you're my friend?"

I'm surprised by her questions. Waiting to hear Little Man's response, it feels as though somebody is pounding on my chest.

"I don't know," Little Man replies.

"You don't know?" Zi crinkles up her nose.

He reaches out his finger and pokes her belly and she squirms away, giggling. "I think Khosi would say yes, your mama can hear us," he says.

"As for me...I hope she's right."

They look up then and see me. Little Man's face breaks out in a happy grin, and Zi charges forward, hurtling towards me, arms outstretched to hug me.

I remember what Mama said not too long ago, how you couldn't change the past. *Now you must look ahead*, she said. *There is only this thing called the future.*

I take a deep breath and go towards it.

ACKNOWLEDGEMENTS

This is a book I wrote because I fell in love with African women—little girls and teenagers and young mothers and grandmothers. I could not possibly have written this book without many lengthy trips to South Africa, where families welcomed me into their homes and treated me like a daughter. Though I am writing in the voice of a young woman whose experiences are so radically different from mine, underneath the exterior differences of culture and language, Khosi has many of the same needs, desires, and fears that I had at fourteen.

Any errors in understanding Zulu culture and language are all mine.

I have so many people to thank. I must first thank my Zulu instructors—Galen Sibanda at Stanford; "Mama" Sandra Sanneh at Yale; and Nelson "Baba" Ntshangase and Mary Gordon at the University of KwaZulu-Natal in Pietermaritzburg. I would also like to thank my academic mentors in African history: Charles Ambler, Iris Berger, Richard Roberts, and Sean Hanretta.

There are many families and individuals whom I have stayed with or spent considerable time with in South Africa. Here is a brief, but not exhaustive, list of people who have been very helpful for me in writing this book: The Nene family from Imbali. Gugu Mofokeng. The Dube clan—Bukhosi, Buke, Dumisani, Leocardia, Phillip, Tsepo, Sikumbuzo, and Fikile. Helen and Ross Musselman. Charmaine, Tony, and Nadine Botto. Henry Trotter. Abby Neely. Thokozile Nguse. Anne and Graham Dominy. Izak and Elma de Vries. John Little Bear and his wife Desray Britz. Stephen Carpenter of the Hilcrest AIDS Centre. Dominic Carlyle Mitchell of Fakisandla Consulting, as well as his sister, who took me around the herbal market in Durban and introduced me to several prominent herbalists. Philippe Denis of Sinomlando. Robyn Hemmens. Berenice Meintjies of Sinani, Survivors of Violence. Kevin and Monique Peterson. Wayne Symington. Marie Odendaal and John Inglis. Dr. Ravi Naidoo and Dr. Bheki Ngcobo, both of the Howard Campus at the University of KwaZulu-Natal. S'the Ndlovu of Izimbali Zesizwe. Dr. Nceba Gqaleni of the Nelson Mandela School of Medicine. Fay and Barney Flett. Hilary Kromberg Inglis and Robert Inglis. Zinhle Thabethe, Xolani Zulu, and Dr. Krista Dong of i-Teach, based at Edendale Hospital. Izak Niehaus of Brunel University. Robin Root of NYU. Richard Steele and Ben Wulfsohn, both homeopathic practitioners in the Durban-Pietermaritzburg region. John Daniels and Elan Lax, both who served on the Truth and Justice Commission. Debbie Mathew of the AIDS Foundation of South Africa. Alan Whiteside of the Health Economics and HIV/AIDS Research Division of Howard Campus, University KwaZulu-Natal. Thulani Zondi, formerly of L'Abri and of i-Teach. Heleen Johnson of the Thusanani Children's Foundation. Trudy Mhlanga from Zimbabwe.

In addition to traveling to South Africa and spending time with a lot of wonderful people, I read a lot of books. There is one scholar whose work proved tremendously helpful: Adam Ashforth. In fact, the direct wording of the sign "Brothers and Sisters, we are abel to cure any sick," comes from one of his books on witchcraft in South Africa. I also appreciated Jonny Steinberg and Helen Epstein's work on AIDS in Africa.

Writer friends Lora, Amanda, Christine, Annemarie, Ann, and my mother Becky all read this book at various stages and offered suggestions that helped. My agent Jennifer Carlson not only helped with the writing and marketing of this book but also introduced me to her husband Andrew Zolli of PopTech, who put me in touch with several very helpful people in South Africa.

Many thanks to the whole Cinco Puntos gang for believing in this work and teaming up with me to create one great book.

Last, but certainly not least, I owe a huge debt of gratitude to my husband, Chris Gibson, who was always supportive and never once complained about the huge chunks of time we spent apart while I was tracking down people and information in South Africa.

GLOSSARY OF ZULU WORDS

The Zulu language is structurally very different from English. It is organized around the noun. There are seventeen classes of nouns. Because the initial part of the noun is dropped when constructing a sentence, it can be difficult for English speakers to look up nouns in a Zulu dictionary. This initial part of a noun may also be dropped when a person is addressed directly. For example, *amantombazana* means "little girls," but if you were addressing a group of little girls directly, you would address them as *Ntombazana*.

Please note that though I have often pluralized words the Zulu way, I have made some exceptions. The plural for *sangoma* should be *izangoma* but I have pluralized it the English way by referring to a group of healers as *sangomas*. I have also done this with the word *tsotsi*.

Amandla	Power, strength. During the war for liberation, black South Africans used this phrase as a rallying cry against the whites in power who suppressed and oppressed them. The response to *Amandla* is *Awethu*, which means "to us."
Amantombazana	Little girls.
Angazi/Angaz'	"I don't know."
Angiguli	"I'm not sick."
Awethu	"To us!" See *Amandla*.
Baba	Father.
Babamkhulu	Grandfather.
Braai	Barbecue, an Afrikaans word.
Cha	"No."
Dagga	Marijuana.
Gogo	Grandmother. Zulus refer to older women as Gogo, even when there is no familial relationship.
Gogo kaThandi	Thandi's grandmother. Literally, grandmother of Thandi.
Hamba/Hambani	"Go!" "Run!" Adding the "ni" to the end makes the word plural.
Hapana	"No."
Hawu	An exclamation like "Wow!"
Hayibo	An expression of disbelief or surprise, similar to *hawu*. It is sometimes spelled *haibo*.
Hhayi	An exclamation, like "No!" or "No way!"
I-dining	The dining room.

Imbali	Literally, the word means "flower," but it is also a township located just outside the city limits of Pietermaritzburg.
Impela	"Indeed."
Impepho	An herb, commonly burned as incense by *sangomas*.
Impi	An army regiment. Can also refer to a family group, e.g., a father, his brothers, and all their sons.
Impundulu	A lightning bird, sent by witches. It is an evil portent, suggesting that you or one of your loved ones has been bewitched.
Indoda	Man.
Intombazana	A little girl who has not yet menstruated.
Intombi	A girl who has reached the age of maturity, that is, one who is capable of bearing children.
Isithunzi (sake)	One's character, personality, or soul. It can also refer to a person's "shadow," the level of goodness and strength within, that turns him or her into an ancestor after their death.
Kwaito	A style of music popular in South African townships—a combination of Afropop and hip-hop.
Lapha	"Here, right here."
Lobola	To pay lobolo.
Lobolo	Bride price.
Makhosi	A term of respect used for sangomas.
Masihambe	"Let's go."
Mfana	Boy. The actual noun is *Umfana*, but Zulu speakers drop the initial "u" sound when addressing somebody directly as "Boy." When Thandi drags out the "a" sound, *Mfaan*, she is just using slang to address her boyfriend as "Boy."

Mina?	"Me?"
Mntwana wam'	"My child."
Muthi	Medicine, all kinds. It can be used to heal somebody or for witchcraft purposes, which include poisoning one's enemies. In popular culture, muti (spelled without the "h") is synonymous with witchcraft potions.
Na mina?	"And as for me?"
Ncese	Shame.
Ndoda	Man. The word is the same as *Indoda* but the initial "i" is dropped when a person is addressed directly as "Man."
Ngena	"Enter."
Ngikhathele kakhulu	"I'm so very tired."
Ngisuthi	"I'm full."
Ngiyabonga	"Thank you."
Ngiyaxolisa	"I'm sorry" or "Forgive me."
Ninjani?	"How are you and your family?"
Ntombazana	A little girl who has not yet menstruated. Without the initial "i," it means the speaker is directly addressing somebody as "Little Girl."
Ntombi	A girl who has reached the age of maturity, that is, she is capable of bearing children. It is the same word as *Intombi* but when a girl is addressed directly as *Intombi*, Zulu speakers drop the initial "i" sound.
Pho!	An exclamation, like "Wow!"
Phuthu	The staple of Zulu meals, a corn meal mush, usually eaten with vegetables and meat.
Rand	South African currency.